MIDWINTER MYSTERIES

A Christmas Crime Anthology

SAPERE
BOOKS

Stories by:
Graham Brack
J C Briggs
Keith Moray
Cora Harrison
Seán Gibbons
Marilyn Todd
Gaynor Torrance
David Field
Kim Fleet
M J Logue
Linda Stratmann

MIDWINTER
MYSTERIES

Published by Sapere Books.

20 Windermere Drive, Leeds, England, LS17 7UZ,
United Kingdom

saperebooks.com

ISBN: 978-1-913335-59-5

Table of Contents

AWAY IN A MANGER BY GRAHAM BRACK

Prague, Czech Republic, 2006

Lieutenant Josef Slonský envied his assistant Jan Navrátil. Navrátil had just returned from Mass and had a peaceful look about him. There was a shiny, well-scrubbed appearance about the face beaming at Slonský across the desk, and he was almost tempted to fling a fist at it to see if he could stop Navrátil smiling.

'One more night, sir,' Navrátil said.

'Is your life expectancy that short? It's all those cinnamon cookies you've been eating.'

'One more night until Christmas,' Navrátil explained.

'Ten out of ten for observation. Unfortunately, peace on earth and goodwill to all men is not the motto of the Prague criminal community, so we can't relax our vigilance just because two thousand years ago an unmarried mother popped her baby in a shed in the Middle East.'

'Stable, sir.'

'I'm glad you are, lad, but that doesn't change anything.'

'The baby, sir — born in a stable.'

Slonský stretched and yawned. 'Well, it all smacks of a shocking lack of foresight to me. Come on, lad, get your coat and we'll go and have a spiced wine to keep the cold out.'

'It's quite warm in here, sir.'

Slonský sighed. The boy could be quite slow sometimes. 'Yes,' he explained as if speaking to a particularly stupid five-year-old, 'but it will be quite cold at the wine stall.'

'Am I invited too, sir?' asked Kristýna Peiperová, who had been keeping quiet in the background. She knew how much the religious side of Christmas mattered to Jan Navrátil, her boyfriend and colleague, whereas she was hoping that the festive season would bring one or two parties, and any excuse to limber up with a glass of wine seemed good to her.

'Of course,' said Slonský, who had completely forgotten that she was there. 'The more the merrier. Though I don't think we'll extend the invitation to Captain Lukas, who tends to take an old-fashioned view to work celebrations.'

The lie had been given to this by the Christmas party that Lukas had sanctioned, apparently unaware that Slonský had only suggested it to Peiperová to give her something to do. Nevertheless, the consensus was that she had done a good job of the planning, and could hardly be held responsible for the small difficulty over Slonský's bar bill.

The three of them, suitably swaddled in their overcoats, marched along the corridor, which took them past Lukas' office. The eponymous captain glanced up and took in the scene at once.

'Going out on patrol, eh? First class. There's a lot of sneak thievery at this time of year. It's good to have plain clothes officers right in the midst of it all, keeping an eye on things.' He glanced at his watch. 'Don't work these young people too hard, Slonský. Why not let them slip off a little early seeing as it's Christmas? You and I can see the shift out, can't we?'

Slonský had never seen himself as a ventriloquist, but somehow managed to speak through clenched teeth. 'Of course, sir.'

'Jolly good.'

Lukas lowered his voice. 'Is Dvorník all right, do you think?'

'So far as I know, sir. Why?'

'He volunteered to do a shift on Christmas Day. I'd have thought that as a family man, he would want to be with his children.'

'All eight of them, sir?'

'Ah — you think that has something…'

'I'm sure of it, sir. The other day, Dvorník spoke approvingly of King Herod's approach to childcare.'

'Ah, quite. Well, don't let me detain you. Get out there and kick some bottoms. That's what they say in American detective films, I think.'

'Very nearly, sir.'

Navrátil and Peiperová wished Lukas a Merry Christmas and followed Slonský down the stairs to the front desk. Sergeant Mucha was, as usual, without his jacket. However, he was also decorated in tinsel, which was definitely not usual.

'Auditioning for a role as a piece of scenery at the National Theatre?' Slonský asked him.

'It's called Christmas spirit. You should try it.'

'The only Christmas spirit I want to try is flavoured with peach or pear and comes in a schnapps bottle. However, Captain Lukas wants us to go out and detect some crime.'

Mucha tutted. 'What is the world coming to, when doing our jobs is allowed to get in the way of drinking? I have half a mind to write to the Director of Police.'

'You have half a mind, full stop,' Slonský replied. 'And I won't hear a word said against the Director, who is a very nice man.'

'Yes, we all know you've met him. And for once it wasn't at a disciplinary hearing.'

'If you're going to be sarky, I won't tell you where we're going and you'll miss out on a Christmas drink at the end of your shift.'

'That would be spiteful, particularly considering that the wife's sister is spending Christmas with us.'

Slonský felt a pang of conscience at having abused the saint standing in front of him. 'You poor beggar. What did you do to deserve that?'

'I don't know,' replied Mucha ruefully, gently rubbing his chin. 'I must have been slow to put my foot down. I think she asked me during a Slavia match and I didn't give her request my full attention. That'll teach me.'

'She did ask, then, before inflicting the Evil Witch of Kutná Hora on you?'

Mucha scratched his head doubtfully. 'I think she must have done. She wouldn't invite her sister for Christmas and not say anything to me about it, would she?'

Slonský clapped him sympathetically on the shoulder. 'Courage, mon brave. We'll be in Old Town Square when you finish. If you can't see us, have a look in one of the bars along Celetná.'

'If I can't see you? In Old Town Square? With the Christmas market on?' cried Mucha.

But he was speaking to a swinging door as Slonský and his ducklings headed out into the snow.

The square was, predictably enough, heaving. There was a jostling sea of humanity that ebbed and flowed according to which particular group of shoppers was able to push hardest, but Slonský, who was taller than average, seemed to know where he was going, so Navrátil, who was shorter than average, trustingly followed. Peiperová, who was tall for a woman, could see Slonský's hat but not much else.

'This way,' bellowed Slonský, barging his way through the crowd.

'Where are we going?' asked Peiperová.

'There's a wine stall over there. That's a good place to start,' Slonský replied.

After some minutes of heaving the trio were reunited in front of the stall, and Slonský, who had arrived first and placed an order, shoved a paper cup of hot, spiced wine in each of their hands.

'I thought Captain Lukas said we were on duty and we were to mingle with the crowd, sir,' Navrátil protested, though he sipped the wine happily first.

'Look around you, young man. Lots of people, and some of them have cups of wine in their hands. What better way of blending in than to do exactly the same? Happy Christmas, by the way.' Slonský took a gulp of wine and spluttered. 'God, that's hot.'

The stall-keeper mutely pointed to the sign reading "Hot Wine".

'Yes, I know,' said Slonský, 'but I thought that was just advertising puffery. After all, it also says "Tasty sausages" and I know better now.'

Peiperová cradled her cup and looked about her. Seeing an unwanted crate, she turned it upside down and stood on it so she could see better. 'Looks peaceful enough. Plenty of city police about, sir. I don't think there'll be much for us to do.'

'Exactly,' said Slonský. 'The perfect place to do your policing, where there are already plenty of other police. But,' he added, 'from another branch of the police so we don't look inefficient.'

'Oh, look!' squealed Peiperová, 'a nativity play. Can we go and watch?'

She was pointing to the end of the square, somewhere near the House at the Stone Bell.

'Yes, run along, children,' Slonský replied, 'but play nicely and don't get kidnapped and sold into white slavery. Especially you, Peiperová — you've got previous on that one.'

This was a reference to Peiperová having been snatched by criminals in the early summer and from anyone else it might have been thought to be in poor taste, but Slonský also had previous, so the comment was overlooked by its recipient who was, in any event, dragging Navrátil through the crowd towards a group of young actors who were, indeed, performing the nativity story. Rather unbiblically, they wore several layers of skiing thermals under their robes, but Prague in December is a very different place from Bethlehem and authenticity had to yield to a natural human desire to stay alive. Not to mention, of course, the difficulty the actors would have had in pronouncing their lines through chattering teeth.

Slonský had seen an old friend standing in front of the Grand Café Praha, and made his way across to greet the journalist, Valentin.

'Are you barred from here too?' Slonský asked cordially.

'I've just come out,' Valentin explained. 'It's like the moon in there — no atmosphere.'

'Yet I detect it took you some time to determine that. Has the gutter press run out of lies to print?'

'Heavens, no. But we're not publishing tomorrow, so I thought I would come out and look for something to write a colour piece on for the St Stephen's Day edition.'

'How about "Latest — Good King Wenceslas looks out"?'

'Very droll. And he wasn't a king anyway. Just a duke.'

'Why this sudden penchant for accuracy? It's never marred your reporting in the past.'

Valentin sighed. 'I'm coming towards the end of my career, Slonský. I've written millions of words, and it suddenly struck me the other day that when I'm gone nobody will remember a single bloody one of them.'

'Intercourse.'

'I beg your pardon?'

'Intercourse. That was one of your words. I read it in a court report you did. I particularly remember because I was surprised you knew the word. Normally you just say…'

'I know what I normally say, but you can't put that in a newspaper. And it doesn't alter the point that the output of a newspaperman is necessarily ephemeral.'

'Come again?'

'It doesn't last. Look at Kafka — pegs out at forty having scribbled a few books, and people study his work incessantly. Or Jaroslav Hašek. He writes *The Good Soldier Švejk* and pops off at thirty-nine, and the damn thing is still in print eighty years later. My words get recycled within days and nobody gives a toss about them.'

'Oh, I don't know,' mused Slonský. 'You've saved some families a fortune in toilet paper.'

Valentin glowered at him. 'Some comfort you are to an old friend undergoing an existentialist crisis.'

'I love it when you talk dirty,' Slonský replied. 'Would you refuse a cup of hot wine?'

Valentin nodded at the cup in Slonský's hand. 'I'd refuse that one. It's muck.'

Slonský peered into the interior. 'Actually, you're right. It's pretty foul, even by street wine standards. Let's go and find something more palatable.'

Valentin drew his coat around himself and stepped into the crowd. 'Where are the kiddies?'

'It's my day to have custody of them,' Slonský told him. 'I sent them away to watch the play. They like theatre. They'll sit happily for hours. It's almost as good as the cinema, though I notice they often can't tell me a damn thing about the film they've allegedly seen.'

They were skirting the edge of the square, when they came upon a uniformed policeman who was being harangued by a middle-aged woman in a ghastly pink suit. Her hair was tinted to match, as could be seen by the portion that was blowing in the breeze as it poked out from under the hood of her jacket.

'Everything in hand, Officer Krob?' asked Slonský.

Krob sprang into a salute, which led the woman to conclude that she now had a superior officer to whom to complain. Since her complaints were in English, a language of which Slonský understood next to nothing, this was even less successful than addressing Krob, who at least knew what she was telling him.

Slonský held his hands up to cajole her into silence and conveyed with hand gestures that he wanted to speak to Krob. Krob reinforced the plan verbally.

'My officer, she wishes to speak to me firstmost,' he explained. The woman, while puzzled, nodded assent, so Krob turned to Slonský. 'This lady has had her purse stolen, sir. She says it happened only five minutes ago and we have to run because the criminal will be getting away.'

'Through this crowd? A confounded serpent would have trouble slithering away through this lot. How does she know it was only five minutes ago?'

Krob asked the question in something approaching English and received a voluble answer. 'She says she bought some postcards and stamps in the shop behind me, and the shop assistant told her she could just catch the next collection at the postbox if she could get them ready in ten minutes. It's now five minutes to the hour, so that must have been five minutes ago.'

Slonský could not fault the logic, though he checked his watch to see if the clocks in sight were accurate. Finding that they were, he asked his next question. 'And she couldn't have left her purse in the shop?'

'We've asked. The assistant says this lady put her purse in her shoulder bag in front of her.'

'Okay. There's damn all chance we'll see it again, but we've got to do something, I suppose.' Slonský took out his mobile phone and called Mucha, asking him to radio all the police in the square to tell them to watch out for sneak thieves.

'As if they aren't already doing that,' said Valentin.

'I know, but now they'll know there really are some,' Slonský responded.

The woman was nodding approvingly and appeared to be telling Krob that if he had telephoned Mucha himself at once, this would be turning out very differently. Krob was placating her as best he could, given that his English was unequal to the task. Having told her that she must not become deranged, he assured her that the Prague police would do all in their power to see that she was reunited with her bucket as quickly as possible, 'if not soonerer'.

There was a certain amount of commotion from the corner of the square where it joined Dlouhá. Climbing onto a chair, Slonský could see a slim, energetic figure in black waving his arms about and directing the erection of barriers at the exits to the square. He reached across to Krob's lapel to speak into his radio. 'Štajnhauzr, is that you?'

'Who's that?' Štajnhauzr replied.

'Who's that, *sir*, you mean. Lieutenant Slonský. What are you doing?'

'We've had a string of complaints of thefts in the last hour. We've been closing off the exits. If need be I'll search every man, woman and child in the square, sir.'

'I admire your ambition, Štajnhauzr, but some of them will die of old age before you get round to them. Stay where you are, and I'll come over to meet you.'

Fending off the American lady's pleadings to him to arrest the entire population of Prague on suspicion, Slonský began to push his way from one side of the square to the other, closely followed by Valentin, who grabbed hold of the belt of Slonský's coat.

'Do you have to do that?' barked the detective.

'I'm a citizen,' Valentin snarled back. 'I'm as entitled to police protection as anyone else. "To help and protect", isn't that your motto? So help and protect me. I may not have much, but what I've got is in my wallet, and if it's going to get stolen I'm going to have the best detective I know a metre away poised to nail the criminal.'

Slonský was quite taken with the description so he dropped the subject and resumed his muscular way. As they traversed the crowd, they caught a glimpse of Peiperová and Navrátil watching the play. Navrátil was having to jump at intervals to see over the crowd in front of him. Peiperová experienced no such difficulty. The Three Kings were moving among the crowd with baskets soliciting donations, presumably for their own pockets. It seemed something of a perversion of the biblical tale where the Kings brought gifts for the infant Jesus, but no doubt they had to fund their pursuit of the Star somehow.

Suddenly Slonský stopped. 'Where's something to stand on?' he snapped.

'Why ask me?' Valentin replied. 'You're taller than I am.'

'But anything to stand on will be on the ground, and you're nearer to it than I am.'

Slonský had spotted an elderly lady sitting on a chair. Waving his police badge, he asked her to stand up for a moment. With difficulty she obliged, and he stepped up to stand on the seat, asking Valentin to hold it steady.

Hopping down, he charged forward with renewed vigour.

'That's very interesting,' was all he said in explanation. Even Valentin's famed investigative skills could not prise more from Slonský's lips until he met up with Štajnhauzr at the corner of the square. By this time Valentin had lost touch, so he heard nothing of the conversation that took place, but was amazed to find the two policemen coming towards him as Štajnhauzr gestured to other policemen to head in various directions.

It took a couple of minutes for all the men to move into position, but finally they were all in place and Štajnhauzr gave the order to move in and arrest their targets. A shocked crowd gasped as the Kings were grabbed by the police and pushed towards the Holy Parents, who were packing up for the journey into Egypt that would take them away from King Herod's clutches.

Following some more shoving, Štajnhauzr and Slonský, pursued by a wheezing Valentin, managed to make their way to the front of the crowd.

A puzzled policeman addressed Slonský. 'They're clean, sir. Nothing on them.'

Slonský was acutely aware of hissing from the crowd who were bewildered by the abrupt break in the performance. He had been so sure that he knew what was happening, but now it looked as if he had it wrong.

Suddenly an idea came into his head. He yelled for Navrátil and Peiperová to join him. The young couple responded with waves to show their presence and came towards him, Peiperová's hand held aloft to show their progress.

'Navrátil,' said Slonský, 'you don't miss much. Is this the first time the Kings have collected money?'

'No,' replied his assistant. 'One or other of them has been around most of the time.'

Slonský took in the scene at a glance, then charged onto the stage area, pushed past Joseph and Mary, and grabbed the innkeeper. He yanked at the sash round his waist and pulled the costume open. To everyone's surprise, there was another costume underneath.

'Four Kings?' said Štajnhauzr.

'That's what I saw,' said Slonský. 'There were only three in the play, but there were four in costume. At any given time three were in sight, but the fourth one was here behind the scenery.'

Shrieks of horror filled the air as Slonský picked up the baby Jesus and threw it to Štajnhauzr. Lifting the manger up, he tipped the contents out and several wallets fell on the snowy ground. With a sharp tug, he pulled the baggage off the donkey and opened it. A trove of glistening electrical items, small purses and credit cards greeted his eyes.

'While we were watching the play, the fourth King collected the stolen items from accomplices in the crowd. He took them round the back and hid them anywhere he could, initially in the manger, but after the Holy Family arrived at the inn he had to stow the rest in their bags. Navrátil, Peiperová, book the entire cast.' Slonský retrieved the doll from Štajnhauzr. 'I think you can let the baby Jesus go,' Slonský said. 'He's innocent, just like the real one.'

It was a long evening, but eventually the Holy Family, Kings, shepherds, King Herod and innkeeper were all under lock and key in the cells. Lukas, who had helped with taking the statements in order to expedite matters, rubbed his weary face and reached for his coat, then, with unexpected nimbleness, ran to the windows and threw them open.

'What are you do—?' Slonský began, but stopped as the sound of church bells filled the room.

'Midnight,' said Lukas. 'Happy Christmas to you all.'

They shook hands, except Navrátil and Peiperová who exchanged a long, lingering kiss. Too late, they realised that officers who work together are not supposed to form "attachments".

Lukas shrugged his coat onto his shoulders, winked at Slonský and announced, 'I saw nothing, did you, Josef?'

'Not a thing, sir.'

'Well, I'm off to my home and bed. A job well done. What are you doing for Christmas, Josef?'

'I thought I might come in and keep Dvorník company for an hour or two.'

'Well, after you've done that, come over for lunch. You know where it is. You two are welcome as well.'

'Thank you, sir, but our mothers are expecting us,' said Navrátil.

'Aren't you spending Christmas Day together?' said Slonský.

'Yes, sir,' Peiperová explained. 'We're having lunch with my parents, then we're driving across to see Navrátil's mother for the evening. It'll mean two Christmas meals, I'm afraid, but we can't let either down.'

Navrátil grimaced. 'It's going to be a long Christmas Day,' he said.

Want more from Slonský and the team?
Start reading the Josef Slonský Investigations series
now!

Connect with Graham Brack!
Facebook/GrahamBrack
Twitter:@GrahamBrack
grahambrackauthor.wordpress.com

FOOTPRINTS IN THE SNOW BY J C BRIGGS

Christmas Eve, London, 1850

Charles Dickens stared out at the snow which lay thick and shining under a great lamp of a moon. The moon seemed unusually large to him, yet it was peaceful, seeming to light the way to the heavens. It must have stopped snowing sometime during the evening. The lawn below his window was perfectly smooth, as if a giant had laid a snow-white cloth for his Christmas feast. Not a mark, not a footprint, not even the faint pencil scratch of a bird. And the silence was profound. The household had gone to bed, worn out by the feasting and dancing.

It had snowed hard and thick for three days and everyone's plans had gone awry, his own included. It was Christmas Eve, and he should have been home in Devonshire Terrace; he should have, as was his custom, taken his children to the toy shop; he should have dined with his guests after at home. But travel home had been impossible for all the visitors at Fareaway Abbey. They had decided to make the best of it, and the impromptu party had been the gayest imaginable. Sir Gaston Fareaway and his wife, Lady Adelina, were the most charming hosts and not a whit put out by their unexpected guests.

The evening had ended with Dickens telling a story.

'A ghost story!' Arthur Fareaway, a good-humoured young gentleman, had cried after the music had ceased and they all sat exhausted by the fire in the great hall where the candles flickered on the Christmas tree.

Sir Gaston had thought it too late, but he was outvoted. All eyes had, of course, turned to Mr Dickens. They had wanted *A Christmas Carol*, but Dickens thought of poor Sir Gaston. The *Carol* was much too long. He looked at the Christmas tree, at the fire, and around the great hall with its black oak panelling and high beamed ceiling. *Improvise then.*

The lamps had been turned down, and by the light of a branched candlestick set upon a table near him, Dickens had begun:

'We come to the house, and it is an old house, full of great chimneys where wood is burnt upon the hearth, and grim portraits — some of them with grim legends, too — lour distrustfully from the oaken panels of the walls…'

His audience had been spellbound; only the fall of ash in the fire and the occasional crack of a log had broken the enchanted silence. Flames leapt up at intervals, and in their light Dickens had seen their rapt faces. The tale came easily to him, and from time to time his eye rested upon a listener who grinned at the entrance of the wicked cavalier, or one who glanced down at the floor when he described the bloodstain which could not be got out. Even Sir Gaston, whose eyes had drooped, opened them and chuckled when he heard of the middle-aged nobleman who had given a generous supper to a houseful of company. Only one face never looked Dickens's way, but looked, it seemed fixedly, across the room. At what or whom, Dickens could not tell.

'And then we go to our bedroom,' Dickens continued. 'It is a very old room. There are great black beams in the ceiling, and there is a great black bedstead, supported at the foot by two great black figures who seem to have come off a couple of old tombs in the old church in the park. At length we go to bed. Well, we can't sleep. The embers on the hearth burn fitfully and make the room look ghostly. And the locked door opens — and there comes in a young woman, deadly pale, and with long fair hair, who glides to the fire, and sits down in the chair, wringing her hands. Our tongue cleaves to the roof of our mouth, and we can't speak. Her clothes are wet; her long hair is dabbled with mud…'

Dickens paused for effect, sensing the combined shiver creeping along the spines of his audience. Several looked up at the ancient timbers of the great hall and thought of the black bedsteads in their rooms. Someone looked at the door as if she thought two black figures might come in from their graves. Dickens looked across to see one white face staring back at him. The eyes seemed to blaze in the firelight, and then the face looked away again into the dark.

'We know that girl; we know those eyes that fix their gaze on us,' Dickens continued, 'and never wink or close. Hush! The blood chills at our heart. The eyes are glassy bright, but we know them well…'

Dickens felt as if his skin burned, that white-hot gaze again, but he dared not return that look. It was time to get rid of that ghost.

'She rises from her seat. She looks about her. We wonder if she seeks someone other than ourselves, and we point to the door with a quivering hand. She nods her head, and wrings her hands again. Then passes the bedside, and goes out of the door which seems to open at her touch. We hurry on our dressing gown and make to follow. The door is closed. The key is in the lock where we left it. We never sleep that night.'

Dickens glanced at the Christmas tree where the candles were going out one by one. He brought his tale to a close: 'O

Christmas tree, let me look once more! I know there are blank spaces on thy branches, where eyes that I have loved have shone and smiled; from which they are departed. But, far above, I see the raiser of the dead girl, and the widow's son; and God is good! Amen.'

There was applause, and a general sense of peace and quiet joyfulness as the company rose to go to their beds. Dickens saw only one thing: that ravaged face and those burning eyes.

An odd fellow, Julius Redlaw — almost mad, Dickens had thought on the morning before the day of Christmas Eve. Redlaw only, of the trapped guests, had wanted to try any which way to leave. Dickens thought now of his agitation. It had seemed excessive, even though he had explained he wanted to get home to his wife who was unwell. Redlaw had begged a horse from Sir Gaston — thinking he could ride to the railway station.

Sir Gaston had turned his eyes to the library window through which could be seen the whirling snow, driven by a bitter east wind. There was no knowing when it would stop, Sir Gaston had pointed out. The very sky was laden with it so that great swags of cloud seemed about to burst with snow. 'Impossible, my dear fellow,' Sir Gaston had declared.

Julius Redlaw's face had been white with anger. It seemed to have shrunk to bone. His hands shook. He said he must walk then. He could not stay. It was imperative he leave — at once.

Dickens attempted to reason with him. 'You'll meet your death out there, sir, and cause your wife more heartache. Don't think of it, I beg you.'

He was rewarded by a look of such blazing fury that he felt scorched.

'What do you know of life or death? Or heartache?' Redlaw snapped.

Enough, Dickens had thought, but he was saved from answering by the timely entrance of Lady Adelina to whom her husband turned for support. Redlaw was apparently soothed by her kindly tone. She promised that as soon as the snow stopped arrangements would be made for his prompt departure, but it was impossible now. Redlaw did not turn on her when she mentioned his wife — politeness forbade that, and at length he was calm and went away to his room.

'Poor Julius,' said Lady Adelina, 'he has always been rather sensitive, and unreasonable. He is, I am afraid, too much wrapped up in himself and his fancied injuries.'

'What about his wife?' asked Dickens, 'is she really so ill?'

'No; a bit of a chill, I think. He fancies her delicate and imagines all kinds of disaster. I rather think it is jealousy. She should have been here, but the chill, it seems, prevented her.'

'Didn't expect him to come,' said Sir Gaston, 'and I wish he could go. A bit of a blight on the proceedings. This damned snow. I beg your pardon, Adelina, my dear, but he is an irritating fellow at the best of times.'

'Alice insisted. I called there last week. I thought she was looking rather wan and tired. She complained that she couldn't sleep. Julius immediately said he would stay with her, but she was adamant that he should come. Said she simply wanted to rest quietly, and that her mother would come to nurse her.'

'A rest from him, I daresay,' Sir Gaston muttered.

'Are they not happy?' ventured Dickens. He could not help being curious at such fury, and then the mention of jealousy.

'I think he is a rather wearing person.' Lady Adelina chose her words carefully. 'He is so highly strung, and she so pretty and sociable. I sometimes think he would like to lock her up in a tower, but Alice is a young woman of character, determined to have a life of her own. Still, there is no doubt he loves her — and I am sure she loves him.'

Dickens had not paid much attention to Julius Redlaw during the dinner and subsequent jollity. He had no wish to speak to the man again. Those burning eyes had unsettled him, as had the curious response to his attempts to reason with him. Well, he had supposed, it hadn't been his business. He ought not to have interfered. Nevertheless, Redlaw's words had stung him.

Looking at that great moon now, Dickens thought, what were his books about if not life, and its dark sister, Death? Yet, who, or what, was it that Redlaw had stared at so fixedly as Dickens told his ghost story?

Ah, well, the clear night promised a brighter day tomorrow, and then Dickens could make his way home. He probably would not meet Julius Redlaw again. He closed his curtains and made ready for bed.

After breakfast, Dickens packed his travelling bag. As he had foretold, the morning upon which he looked out was bright and clear. Someone had been out already. There was a clear set of footprints across the snowy grass. The coach which was to take the guests to the station was already at the door, and the footman was stacking boxes and portmanteaux. Dickens heard voices. People were making ready to depart. It was time he went down. Then he heard the lightest of knocks at his door.

Sir Gaston came in. He looked pale and anxious.

Dickens said, 'Oh, am I keeping everyone? I am ready to go.'

Sir Gaston put a finger to his lips and spoke unusually quietly. 'Can you wait a while, Mr Dickens? Could you take the afternoon train? I think we may need your help.'

'Certainly, what may I do for you?'

'It's Redlaw. He's locked himself in his room. Hasn't been down for breakfast and the footman can't get an answer. I've told him I'll deal with it. I rather hope you might...'

'You think something's wrong?' Dickens asked.

'I do. I stood at the door. There's a silence. It's as if I were knocking at the door of an empty room.'

'Do you think he's gone already? There are footprints across the lawn. Perhaps he didn't want to wait — has walked to the station. He seemed so agitated last night. I noticed how distracted he was during my story.'

'Fool thing to do if he has. There's only the one train this morning. My coach would have been just as quick. But, no, he can't have — the door's locked from the inside. The key's in the lock.'

'Window?' Dickens went to look out of his. 'He could have jumped. Look, the snow is very deep against the walls and on the path. He wouldn't have come to any harm — be like landing on a cushion. He did seem desperate.'

'I don't know — I'll have to go out and look under his window. Mad thing to do if he did — but then I never thought he was very stable. Do you mind waiting until the coach has gone? If there is something wrong, I'd rather —'

'I understand.'

'I'll go and see the others off and check beneath the window. Perhaps you could listen at his door?'

Dickens followed Sir Gaston, who went downstairs after pointing out the door at the end of the corridor. Dickens knocked lightly. But there was no sound within. He did not dare knock too loudly. That might bring a servant, and Sir Gaston wanted secrecy — at least for the time being. He put his ear to the door, but there was nothing to hear.

He knocked again and understood what Sir Gaston had felt. It did seem as though he were knocking at an empty room. The man was gone... Or worse? He thought of that white face and the glittering eyes. Unstable, Sir Gaston had said. A madman, Dickens thought. Perhaps something had turned his abnormal sensitivity into madness. It happened. Something long repressed breaks out — jealousy, he wondered. Redlaw's separation from his wife — the wife who had been adamant for his coming here. Perhaps there was something amiss in that relationship. And the snow which had delayed his departure had been the tipping point.

Dickens listened again, feeling more and more apprehensive. He thought about that fixed gaze. He wondered what the man had been looking at. Nothing, he supposed. Whatever it was, it had been in his mind's eye. Perhaps he had been imagining his wife at home with some other man. And at the end of the story, how Redlaw's eyes had blazed at Dickens's final blessing.

He started at the sound of footsteps. Sir Gaston came puffing up the stairs and along to the door.

'Anything?' Sir Gaston asked.

'Not a sound. The window?'

'Shut fast and the curtains still closed. And the snow is not the least disturbed. It would have been had he jumped. There were only the footprints — a woman, I'd say. One of the servants out early.'

'Then we have to get in.'

'Not break down the door?'

'Have you a man who could somehow force the door without too much noise?'

'Couldn't you?'

'I'll need tools — a chisel, a hammer. Can you get those?'

28

'I don't suppose I can. I'll have to get Giles. He'll be discreet.'

Dickens waited again. It seemed a long time — a long, silent time during which he knocked lightly again, a long silent time in which he became certain that the man was dead — had killed himself. There could be no other explanation.

Giles, the butler, came with the tools, and managed to dismantle the lock and prise open the door. He stood back and Dickens went in. The fire had died out. Redlaw lay on the great black bedstead under the great black beams. His throat was cut. Blood had cascaded from the wound and had soaked the white nightshirt and the counterpane. The smell was of the slaughterhouse.

Dickens felt the bile rise in his throat, but he forced himself to look. He heard Sir Gaston's gasp behind him. Giles shouted out. Dickens saw that the left hand flopped down by the bed. A bloodied cut-throat razor had dropped from that hand.

Sir Gaston cried out, 'Good God! What has he done?' He held on to the bed post and turned his head away.

Giles, whose face had taken on a sickly pallor, retained sufficient command of himself to lead his master to a chair.

Dickens leant over the body. First he closed the eyes, dulled now, but still retaining that horrible fixed expression of madness. He could not bear to look at those eyes again. But he looked at the wound. He had seen something similar before. His policeman friend, Superintendent Sam Jones, had shown him how to examine such a wound. He could see that it was deeper on the right side where the razor had gone in and that it terminated gradually to a sharp angle on the left where only the skin was wounded. He looked at the hand which had dropped from the bed, and the razor which lay there — the left hand. Surely, Redlaw had done this himself. He had to ask.

'Sir Gaston, was Redlaw left-handed?'

Sir Gaston looked a hundred years older than the man who had chuckled at the story last night, but he uttered a hoarse, 'Yes.'

'Then it is suicide, I'm sure.'

Dickens turned back to the body. He stretched out his own left hand and passed it from right to left over the bloody gash. A left-handed murderer could have done it, but it was impossible that a left-handed murderer had left a locked room. Neither could any assassin have jumped from the window, for Sir Gaston had seen no evidence of such an act in the snow. Dickens glanced round the room. There was another door at the side of the bedhead.

'Where does that door lead?' he asked.

Giles answered, 'Just to a small antechamber, sir, but it's never opened — it has no communication with any other part of the house.'

'Please check, Mr Giles, just in case.'

The door was locked. No one could have gone out that way.

The doctor was summoned and a footman sent with a message for the police in the nearest town. Dickens agreed to go to Mrs Redlaw's house in London. He would return if the police wanted him. It was imperative that Alice Redlaw was informed as soon as possible — before news could reach her from any other source. Sir Gaston and Lady Adelina were clearly in no state to go. Sir Gaston had broken down at the sight of that bloody corpse, and his wife, though shattered herself, had much to do to restore him. Dickens offered and Lady Adelina looked upon him as a drowning woman might look upon a man with a life-belt.

The Redlaw house in Portland Street was in complete darkness. Dickens knocked and knocked, but no one came. Perhaps Redlaw's wife had left him. Perhaps there was a lover and Redlaw had known he had lost her. *Don't jump to conclusions*, Dickens chided himself, *don't accuse the poor woman* — who did not know yet that she was a widow. There was a simpler explanation. Her illness had worsened, and her mother had taken her home. Lady Adelina had given him the address. He would go there.

Lady Margaret Bowley, cousin to Lady Adelina Fareaway, explained that of course there could be no answer at Portland Street. Her daughter and son-in-law were in the country at Fareaway Abbey, the house of Sir Gaston Fareaway. Mr Redlaw had persuaded his wife to go even though she had not felt well — Alice found it hard to deny her husband. She had the note from Mr Redlaw telling her that she need not go to Portland Street. News of the heavy snowfalls had reached her. She had guessed that they were delayed. They were to come straight to her from the Abbey for Christmas, or certainly when the snow cleared and it was possible to travel. Their house had been closed, the servants given a holiday.

Dickens had great difficulty in making her understand that Julius Redlaw was dead and that his wife had not been to Fareaway Abbey. He made her stay where she was. He would take his friend, Superintendent Jones of Bow Street, to Portland Street to find out more. He would come back with news as soon as he could.

Alice Redlaw was dead in her bed, her long fair hair dabbled with blood. Her throat had been cut. Superintendent Jones thought that the weapon had been a cut-throat razor. The wound was from right to left, but it did not terminate gradually. It was deeply incised in the soft parts. *Murder.* The murderer had been left-handed. There was no sign of the razor.

Dickens let himself into a silent house. Christmas night was over, and all his guests had gone. His wife and children had retired to bed to sleep their innocent sleep. He was bone-weary and did not want to speak to anyone. He would sleep in his dressing room.

When he closed his eyes, he saw a white face and a pair of burning eyes. Exactly as they had blazed at him. Three times. He sat bolt upright. When had it happened first in the story telling? It was at the moment he had first paused. It was not the black beams or the black bedstead which had enflamed those eyes. It was the ghost woman with the long fair hair dabbled with mud who enters the bedroom and sits down wringing her hands. Mud. Had Redlaw heard blood? Had Dickens's story, so fatefully invented, propelled Julius Redlaw to his final act of madness?

The raiser of the dead girl — had Redlaw seen Alice Redlaw's ghost in the shadows? Had he, in his mania, seen the wife he had murdered enter his bedroom?

Dickens thought of the footprints in the snow. *The footprints of a woman.*

The clock in the hall struck three. Charles Dickens did not sleep again that night.

Want to solve more mysteries with Charles Dickens and Superintendent Jones?
Start reading the Charles Dickens Investigations series now!

Connect with J C Briggs!
Facebook/JCBriggsBooks
Twitter:@JeanCBriggs
jcbriggsbooks.com

LOST AND FOUND BY KEITH MORAY

West Uist, Scotland, 2012

The skirl of the pipes reverberated throughout St Ninian's manse, overpowering all other sound for human ears. Nonetheless, for the umpteenth time Crusoe, Torquil McKinnon's collie, rose from his basket in the kitchen and ran barking down the hall. He launched himself the last three feet and thumped the door panel with his front paws. He continued to bark.

'Crusoe, hold your wheesht, will you?' called Torquil's uncle, affectionately nicknamed the Padre, coming out of the sitting room and following on his heels. 'It's a party and these are guests, not intruders.'

The Padre opened the front door and beamed at the young woman standing in the rain, cradling a bottle in one arm and holding an open umbrella in the other.

'Lorna! *Ceud mìle fàilte*, a hundred thousand welcomes. Come away in out of the sleet and the rain this instant. As you can hear, your fiancé is in full swing. Poor you, having to hold the fort until now.'

He shut the door after her and accepted the bottle she handed him as she collapsed her umbrella and shook the rain off it.

'It was my duty day, Padre,' Sergeant Lorna Golspie replied. 'But I've left Ewan to lock up the station, and Morag is covering this evening.' Popping her umbrella in the stand, she peeled off her coat and hung it up. 'I'll just take my boots off so I don't trail slush in. I wouldn't want to spoil the hall,' she said with a wry smile, nodding at the golf bags full of muddy clubs leaning against the wall, and the line of oil-stained newspapers which protected the parquet floor from the assortment of carburettor components, oil filters and gears that had been there for as long as she had been on West Uist. Torquil had explained to her on her very first visit that they were all part of the ongoing project to rebuild an Excelsior Talisman Twin Sports motorcycle that he and his uncle, the Reverend Lachlan McKinnon, were engaged in.

The Padre's eyes twinkled and he grinned. 'Aye, I ken what you mean. Torquil and I will have to make a New Year's resolution to finish the motorcycle and tidy this up. But this is a Boxing Day party, Lorna, so make yourself comfortable and I'll get —'

The bagpipes stopped, to be replaced by the sound of hearty applause. Almost immediately, music started up again from the unmistakable sounds of a piano accordion and accompanying banjo, tin whistle and fiddle. A moment later Torquil McKinnon, the local police inspector, came out, his pipes under his arm. His hawk-like features burst into a grin, and he ran past his uncle and scooped his sergeant up in his other arm.

'I know just the spot I wanted to show you, Lorna,' he said, walking backwards with her to stop underneath the large bunch of mistletoe hanging from the ceiling.

'Och, come on Crusoe,' the Padre said to the dog. 'We're just a pair of gooseberries here. We'll leave these good representatives of the police to their pagan ritual.'

Inspector McKinnon didn't reply. He was too busy kissing his sergeant.

A ceilidh was going strong in the manse sitting room with about twenty guests either dancing the Gay Gordons or standing well back, laughing, chatting and drinking. A huge Christmas tree decorated with baubles and McKinnon tartan streamers occupied the bay window space, and sitting in front of it were three musicians: an elderly weather-beaten man playing the accordion, a younger man in his mid-thirties playing a banjo and a well-dressed woman in her forties playing a fiddle. An attractive younger woman with shoulder-length blonde hair was standing playing a tin whistle.

Torquil grabbed Lorna's hand and they joined the dancers.

'This gives everyone's ears a wee rest from the bagpipes,' he said, spinning her round. 'Was all quiet on the western front, by the way?'

'Not a thing today, as you'd expect. It was just the same before Christmas. I imagine it will pick up dramatically at Hogmanay.'

'Aye, well that's part of the reason we always have our ceilidh on Boxing Day.' Torquil nodded at the musicians. 'Behold the other members of the Hogmanay Dip and Nip committee. I'll introduce you later, once the dancing stops. They'll be doing an Eightsome reel next and then the Padre's favourite, the McKinnon Jig. He composed it himself and he'll play his pipes with the band.'

Lorna grinned and pointed down at her bare feet. 'I'll need to watch out for any errant clodhoppers then, as well as guard my ears.'

Later, after the music stopped and the guests started to take their leave and were seen out by the Padre, Torquil introduced Lorna to the musicians.

'Folks, I'd like to introduce you all to Lorna Golspie, my sergeant and my fiancée.'

'A pleasure, lassie,' said the weather-beaten accordion player. 'I'm Murdo McTavish.'

'Everyone knows Murdo as Skipper,' Torquil explained. 'He was a fisherman and captained *The Duke's Pride*. He lives in the old Second World War pillbox on the headland along the coast.'

'Ah, I wondered who lived in that pillbox,' Lorna said. 'I like the way it's been preserved and another section added on. A real piece of island history.'

The younger man who had been playing the banjo harrumphed. 'And so is Skipper, too.' He smiled and held out his hand to Lorna. 'I'm Alistair McDonald.' Then, reaching into a jacket, he produced a business card. 'Antiques, bric-a-brac, rare books. If you need any, I'm your man.'

'Pleased to meet you, Lorna,' said the smartly dressed woman. 'I'm Ailsa Ross, the Kyleshiffin Museum curator. I'm afraid I haven't got a card to offer you, but if you'd like to pop into the museum anytime I'd be pleased to show you around the collections.'

'Ailsa is a writer as well as a curator,' Torquil interjected. 'She's an expert on folklore. What she doesn't know about folk medicine and local customs just isn't worth knowing.'

'And that just leaves me, Lorna,' said the young woman with the tin whistle. 'I'm Catriona Beatson. I'm a teacher at Kyleshiffin School.' She raised her tin whistle. 'It's my life's aim to make sure that all children that I have the pleasure to teach learn to play an instrument.'

'She's my great-niece, actually,' added Murdo, reaching down for a glass of whisky under his chair. He took a sip. 'And she's teaching them all to swim as well. Everybody should be able to swim in my opinion. I spent my life out on *The Duke's Pride*, like my father afore me, and many is the tumble I had in the water.'

'But you're still here, Skipper,' said Torquil. 'You were obviously a good enough swimmer.'

Murdo laughed. 'I was drown-proof, actually. My old dad saw to that when he gave me this.' Opening the neck of his shirt, he pulled out a small brass cylinder that hung from a chain, like a medallion. 'This is a lucky cartridge that my grandfather had on him during the Great War. He was in the merchant navy, and he sailed in two ships that were torpedoed. Both times, he was adrift in the water for hours. It was the contents of this shell that saved him, no doubt about it.'

'Because of a bullet?' Lorna queried.

'Inside it is a baby's caul,' Murdo said, tapping the side of his nose knowingly.

Ailsa Ross clicked her tongue and gave a soft chuckle. 'Very rarely a baby is born with a membrane over its head and face, like a veil. Folk used to believe that a baby born with such a caul would never drown and that owning one would protect them from drowning. Sailors would pay a fortune to buy one.'

Murdo replaced his cartridge shell back inside his shirt. 'My grandfather gave it to my father when he went to sea, and he gave it to me. So you see, I'm protected from both drowning and from being shot.' He tossed his head back and laughed heartily. Suddenly, he clapped a hand to his chest as beads of perspiration formed rapidly on his brow.

'Skipper, are you OK?' Torquil asked.

Murdo shook his head, and with a trembling hand he reached into his trouser pocket and pulled out a small silver box. From it he took out a white pill and popped it under his tongue. Moments later, the perspiration had gone and he was grinning again. 'The sea and bullets won't get me, but this bloody angina might.'

Catriona tapped Murdo's arm with her tin whistle. 'Don't tempt providence like that, Skipper.'

'I don't buy into superstitious stuff myself,' said Alistair, 'but am I right in thinking that you have a snuffbox that you're using for your pills?'

'It is that,' Murdo replied, holding it up so they could all see that on the lid was a small ivory profile of a man with a cravat and wig. 'This is even older and has been in my family since the victory at Culloden.'

Alistair harrumphed again. 'The '45 rising was a long time ago, but I see that the McTavish clan still revere Butcher Cumberland.'

Murdo smiled humourlessly. 'I'll not rise to that, Alistair McDonald. The Duke of Cumberland gave all the non-commissioned officers under his command snuffboxes as thanks for their service to King and Country. My family were always proud of him and his allegiance to the true crown. That's why our boat was called *The Duke's Pride.*'

'Some of my ancestors fell fighting for Bonnie Prince Charlie at Culloden in 1746,' said Alistair coldly. 'May I see your box?'

'You can, but before you say anything, it's not for sale.'

The Padre came back in as Alistair was examining the snuffbox. He clapped his hands. 'Now, is everyone ready for the Hogmanay Dip and Nip?'

'What on earth is this Dip and Nip?' Lorna asked.

'Another of the island's quaint customs,' Ailsa explained. 'It started back in the nineteenth century, when the island had a fair-sized fishing fleet and contributed substantially to the herring industry. At New Year, the locals process around the town by torchlight, playing music.'

'That's us,' said the Padre. 'Torquil and myself leading with the pipes, then the Dip and Nip band here, then everyone else.'

Ailsa went on. 'We arrive at the harbour a wee bit before midnight, when the Padre leads us in prayer, just like generations of clergymen before him, then he blesses all the boats that sail from the island and we see out the old year and welcome in the new one.'

'I can understand about the Nip, but what is the Dip?' Lorna asked.

Ailsa beamed. 'It might sound a bit pagan, but a maid takes the plunge into the harbour and swims across. For many years we didn't have any volunteers, for obvious reasons, so one of the young men would don a wig, cover himself in grease and do the honours. But this year, we have a volunteer.'

'Me!' said Catriona proudly.

'Goodness, you're brave,' gasped Lorna. 'It'll be pitch black and cold as ice.'

'Everyone has a hip flask, and believe me the nip after the dip soon warms you up. I've done it twice as a substitute maid after I've played the pipes,' said Torquil. 'Then once the maid is all dried off, we go first-footing to anyone's house that has its lights on.'

Sergeant Morag Driscoll was called out just after seven the next morning by Dr Kevin Henderson, a young newly qualified GP who was doing a locum for Dr Ralph McLelland, the resident Kyleshiffin doctor. He had been contacted by Jimmy Duncan, one of the young lads who delivered the *West Uist Chronicle*.

Sunrise was not until after nine o'clock, so it was still dark. The cold outside temperature and the driving sleet made the purpose of the call doubly miserable.

'It looks like he died from a cardiac arrest, Sergeant Driscoll,' the doctor explained as they stood in the front room of the pillbox, looking down at the body of Skipper Murdo McTavish.

The old fisherman was slumped back in his chair, an expression of agony fixed on his face. In front of him was a cold bowl of porridge with an unused spoon beside it and a salt cellar lying on its side. A number of small white tablets lay scattered over the gingham tablecloth.

'It looks like he had an angina attack, tried to get his glyceryl trinitrate tablets, they're for angina you see, but dropped them all over. Look, there are some on the floor.'

'And Jimmy Duncan found him when he came to deliver his newspaper and called you?'

'He did, the smart lad. I sent him home, because he'll have been shocked finding a body.' The doctor clicked his tongue. 'The reason I called you, though, is that I am not in a position to sign a death certificate. I had no personal knowledge of him, and according to the case notes he'd not been seen by a doctor for months.'

'So it will be a Procurator Fiscal case and possibly a post-mortem?'

'I think so. All very tricky you see, with me just being a locum while Ralph McLelland is away.'

Morag sighed. 'Poor Skipper. Dying alone after Christmas.'

Police Constable Ewan McPhee, the six-foot-four, red-headed, hammer-throwing champion of the Western Isles had opened the station and brewed a pot of tea in readiness for the appearance of his superior officers.

Morag immediately filled him in about her early morning call. 'I'd better get on with the report for the Procurator Fiscal, so I'll be in the rest room if you need me.'

'Poor old Skipper. Will it be a post-mortem then?'

'Aye, which will mean we'll have to get the body over to the mainland, as Dr McLelland isn't here. His locum is a trained GP, but he is not a qualified pathologist like Ralph.' She turned to go. 'Is there tea on the go?'

'It's ready for you, Morag.'

'Have you had any customers yet?'

Ewan grinned. 'A visit from our esteemed editor of the *West Uist Chronicle*. He was sniffing for news items as usual and brought in something for the lost and found cupboard, so I gave him the whole list. He said he'd print it and also put it up on the *Chronicle*'s website. Cora and he had been up late getting the next issue ready, and he was out early for milk and butteries from Allardyce the Baker.'

It was still dark when Torquil and Lorna arrived half an hour later.

'The boss picked me up, Ewan,' she explained, stifling a yawn. 'I wouldn't care if we had a decent amount of daylight this time of the year. Still dark when you get to work and dark for a couple of hours before we get home. I'm permanently tired.'

Ewan had been politely waiting to interrupt the banter. 'There's tea made and Morag is through doing a report for the Fiscal. I'm sorry to tell you, but poor Skipper Murdo McTavish died this morning while he was at his breakfast.'

'Oh, that's bad news,' said Torquil. 'He had a bit of a turn at our ceilidh last night.'

Morag came through at the sound of their voices. 'Sorry, boss. I know Skipper should have been playing at the Hogmanay Dip and Nip. He's done that as long as I can remember.'

'Where's his body?'

'At Mathieson the undertaker's until we know what the Fiscal wants doing. I've taken care of the pillbox and locked it up.'

Torquil nodded. 'The sad end of a tradition, then. We'll just need to make sure that this Hogmanay we give his memory a good send-off. I'll ring the Padre and then Calum at the *Chronicle*. He'll want to put an announcement in the next paper.' He sighed. 'And then I'll call all the others in the band. They're all sure to be shocked.'

The next day brought more surprise. Ewan arrived in the morning to find a back window of the Kyleshiffin Police Station had been jemmied open.

'Broken into!' Torquil exclaimed when he arrived after a high-speed dash on the Bullet from the manse. 'Has anything been taken? Notes, files or personal items?'

'I'm afraid that your office has been ransacked, Torquil. And the fridge was left open and there is milk all over the place.'

Torquil stepped quickly to his office door and peered in. 'We'd better get Morag to dust everywhere for fingerprints when she gets in.'

'Do you think it was kids, Torquil?' Ewan asked doubtfully.

Before Torquil could reply, the front office bell was rung and Ewan went through.

'What's the emergency, Ewan?' Calum Steele asked, his eyes gleaming enthusiastically. He was wearing his trademark yellow anorak and was chewing a freshly baked mutton pie. 'I saw Torquil screech up the Harbour Road.'

Torquil came out. 'We've been broken into, Calum. But don't make too much of it. It's a bit —'

'Embarrassing? I'm sure it is,' the *West Uist Chronicle* editor said, producing his iPhone with the dexterity of a magician. ' "The Kyleshiffin Police Station Burgled!" Can I see where they came in? What have they taken?'

Torquil shook his head. 'No pictures of the crime scene. And I'd rather you just say broken into rather than burgled. Nothing's been stolen. So far, it seems just wanton damage.'

Ewan had taken the opportunity to slip on a rubber glove and gingerly open the cupboards behind the counter. 'I think you might need to change that to burglary, boss. The Lost and Found cupboard has been emptied.'

'That's interesting, Torquil,' said Calum. 'Of course, I have a personal interest in this story now, considering that I was doing my civic duty yesterday morning and brought in an item or two.'

The door opened and Lorna and Morag came in. Lorna was collapsing her umbrella and shaking it out.

Torquil rapidly explained about the break-in.

'Has anything been taken, boss?' Morag asked, coming around the counter.

'Only the Lost and Found items. So we'll need everywhere fingerprinting, starting with the cupboard.' Then of the journalist, he asked: 'And what was it that you brought in yesterday, Calum?'

'It looked like a snuffbox, but it had a couple of pills in it. I was coming out of Allardyce the Baker's yesterday morning, and I saw this cyclist at the end of the road skid in the slush. I shouted and went to help, but whoever it was just climbed on and peddled off up Lady's Wynd. I saw that something had been dropped and I tried to call the person back, but they

44

couldn't have heard. If I had been near my scooter, I would've shot after —'

'Describe this snuffbox, Calum?' Torquil interjected.

Calum held up the remaining quarter of his mutton pie. 'Not very big. About this size, silver with an ivory head on it.'

'And did you put it on the *West Uist Chronicle* website?'

'Aye, I told Ewan I would. Our newspaper is the people's main source of —'

'Thank you, Calum. We'll need to get on,' said Torquil. 'Just go easy on the break-in.'

'The burglary, you mean,' the newspaperman corrected.

'Aye, if you must.'

Later that morning, after the fingerprinting was done and the mess cleared up, Torquil and his team sat in his office going over the list of the Lost and Found in the ledger. In total there were thirteen items, including a wallet, a purse, various bunches of keys, a bag of golf balls and a medical box.

'I assumed it was a medical box,' said Ewan. 'Calum rattled it and opened it to show the pills inside, and I entered it as such.'

'What were the pills like?' Morag asked.

'Wee white ones.'

'It sounds like Murdo's snuffbox,' said Torquil. 'He used it for his pills.'

'It had the head of the Duke of Cumberland on it,' added Lorna. 'Was there anything like that at Murdo's, Morag?'

The sergeant shook her head. 'There were little pills scattered about the table and floor. Doctor Henderson said they were pills for his angina. Glyceryl trinitrate.'

Torquil slapped his hand on the desk. 'Then one thing is clear. Someone took it from Murdo's house.' He looked down the list one final time, then leaped up. 'His body is at the undertaker's, you said, Ewan?'

'Aye, boss.'

'We need to see Murdo's body. And then I need to have a look in the pillbox myself. Ewan, you're in charge of the shop. Come on ladies, we have work to do.'

Morag sent in her initial report to the Procurator Fiscal, who arranged for a post-mortem examination to take place on the mainland the following day.

Torquil took the post-mortem report over the phone the day after that, the 30th December.

'The pathologist reported that the death was a clear-cut case of sudden cardiac arrest as the result of an acute myocardial infarction. There was extensive arteriosclerosis or hardening of the arteries. Nothing suspicious.'

Lorna tapped her fingers on the arm of her chair. 'But yet someone was in his house and took the snuffbox that he used for his pills.'

Morag sipped her tea. 'Aye, and when we went back to the pillbox he lived in, we saw that Murdo hadn't had his porridge, but he had tipped his salt over, presumably when he'd been fumbling for his tablets.'

'Which tells us something about who that person was,' agreed Torquil. 'And apart from Lorna and I, we have three people who saw that snuffbox at the ceilidh on Boxing day.' He reached for his telephone. 'So now it's time to arrange a meeting of the Hogmanay Dip and Nip committee to consider how we are going to handle the ceremony in remembrance of Murdo Mathieson.' He pursed his lips. 'I'll ask them to meet Lorna and I at Murdo's pillbox.'

It was mid-afternoon, and the sleet and the wind were battering the small windows when the musicians met Torquil in the Skipper's converted Second World War pillbox.

The pillbox sat on the headland. It consisted of the original hexagonal pillbox to which an additional cabin-like section with one-foot-thick walls had been added in keeping with the original building. It had three small rooms only, a bathroom built into the actual pillbox, while the sitting room with fine views to the sea, and a kitchen were housed in the cabin extension. The exterior had all been whitewashed so that the add-on part did not seem at all incongruous. The interior was functional rather than comfortable, yet with its nets and floats and lobster baskets around the walls it was clear that it had been the home of a fisherman.

'So sad to be standing in Murdo's house like this,' said Catriona. 'You can almost feel his presence.'

'I've never been to his house before,' said Ailsa.

'It's simple, just like Murdo,' observed Alistair. 'A bit weird to have a meeting here, though. Why's that, Torquil? And why did you want us to bring our instruments? Surely we don't need to have a rehearsal here?'

'Well, I just wanted you all here so I could show you something.' He reached into his pocket and produced Murdo's snuffbox. He rattled it. 'He used it for his pills, as you will all remember.'

'He had a slight turn at the ceilidh, poor man,' said Ailsa. 'He took a pill from there.'

'It's a fine piece,' said Alistair. 'If it wasn't a Cumberland relic, I might have made him an offer for it.'

'Why do you want to show us it, Inspector?' asked Catriona.

There was a knock at the door and Lorna came in, struggling to collapse her umbrella behind her. She closed the door with her rear and stood struggling. 'Sorry I'm late, Torquil. I walked and the wind has blown my umbrella inside out. I just need to adjust it.'

'Oh, you should never open an umbrella indoors,' said Catriona, looking slightly horrified. 'It's bad luck.'

Ailsa nodded agreement. 'This house has seen enough of that.'

Lorna set the umbrella against the wall and muttered apologies.

'As I was about to say,' went on Torquil, 'the snuffbox was lost, but now it's been found. The Padre actually found it and the other lost items taken from the police station in the porch of St Ninians Church, and there was an envelope with it stuffed with five pound notes, fresh from a cash machine. We checked and there were no fingerprints. Just as there were no fingerprints here or at the burglary at the station. Apart from the police officers' prints, of course.'

'It was the second time the snuffbox had been lost and found, you see,' said Lorna. 'The first time was when it was taken from here the morning Murdo died.'

'What are you saying?' Catriona asked.

'Someone took it,' said Torquil. 'One of the five of us here in this room.'

'You are saying one of us is a thief?' snapped Alistair.

'That's outrageous,' agreed Ailsa.

'But what is the reason for the money?' Catriona asked.

Torquil smiled. 'Ah, good question. We think because the person was showing that they weren't a thief. They didn't really want the snuffbox at all. They had just dropped it by accident, and it happened to get picked up by the newspaper editor, Calum Steele. He handed it to PC Ewan McPhee that morning and then put it up on his website as having been lost. The person who lost it saw that on the website and needed to retrieve it, which was why the break-in at the station happened that night.'

'This makes no sense,' said Alistair irritably. 'Why would anyone want it so badly?'

'At first, we thought it could be someone who wanted it to sell on, or to possess as an interesting folklore curiosity, either in a museum or a personal collection,' said Torquil, looking around the room at the members of the Dip and Nip band. 'Then we thought they possibly didn't want it at all. The person really wanted the other thing that Murdo showed us at the ceilidh. His cartridge shell containing the caul.'

Torquil waited and watched them for a moment before continuing, 'We checked with the undertaker, and it was not on the body when he collected it. There was no sign of it here in Murdo's home. No, the snuffbox was taken as a distraction in case whoever found the body had any knowledge about the caul in its brass cartridge and noticed that it was missing. Then when this person tumbled off their bicycle and dropped the thing, they panicked and felt they had to go through with the supposed burglary, so that the snuffbox would remain "lost". They believed that if it was found, then the distraction would be removed and we would focus on the cartridge containing the caul. All very complicated, but now we have a good idea what sort of person that was.'

'Now you are being totally obtuse,' said Ailsa.

'Perhaps, but look at that table. That was where Murdo was about to have his porridge. We've cleared everything away, of course, but all was photographed as we found it. He spilled salt as he fumbled for his tablets and died. Well, whoever was here saw that and tossed some over their shoulder. We found it in the corner there. It couldn't have been Murdo, but it was someone who was standing there, where you are, Alistair.'

The antique dealer looked mortified. 'I did no such thing.'

'No, you didn't,' said Torquil. 'Whoever did this was someone incredibly superstitious, like Murdo himself. Someone who tosses spilt salt over their shoulder.'

'And who is frightened by umbrellas being put up indoors,' added Lorna. 'That was our little test when I came in the door a few minutes ago.'

Torquil turned to the school teacher. 'You wanted that caul at any cost, Catriona, didn't you? You came here the morning after the ceilidh with the intention of buying the caul, but sadly, I imagine Murdo was already dead.' He pointed at the tin whistle that she had been clenching and turning round and round in her hands. 'Play something for us.'

'I … I don't want to!'

Torquil took it from her. 'I thought not. I didn't think you'd want to leave the caul anywhere that it could be found, certainly you didn't plan to wear it here, so —' He upended the tin whistle and tapped, allowing the brass cartridge and chain to flow out into his palm.

Catriona collapsed into a chair and covered her face with her hands. 'I … I meant no harm, but I've been terrified about this Hogmanay Dip and Nip thing ever since I was talked into being the maiden. You see, I'm petrified of water. I don't want to drown, but I'm sure I could if I don't have protection. It … it all happened, just like you said. I was hoping I could persuade him to let me borrow it, because … because he's my great-uncle and it was him that persuaded me to be the Kyleshiffin maid in the first place. Only, he … he was dead when I arrived.

'I panicked, right enough, and took the cartridge and the snuffbox that he'd dropped on the table and I slid off into the dark. And then coming down the hill, my bike slid in the slush and I lost it. I saw Calum Steel coming towards me and I panicked again. Then later I ... I broke into the station and took all the lost things, because I thought if you found the snuffbox, then I would be lost. You are right, I thought it would be like tempting providence to risk letting you focus on the found snuffbox.' She sobbed. 'I'm so sorry.'

The others mumbled various things, and Torquil put a hand on her shoulder. 'We know you are, Catriona. That's why you left the snuffbox and the other things at the church with the money. The question is, what do we do about it?'

The Hogmanay Dip and Nip proceeded better than expected since the whole island had mourned the sudden death of Skipper Murdo McTavish and seemed to have turned out to support the procession. Torquil and the Padre playing the pipes, accompanied by the other members of the Dip and Nip band, had led the torchlight procession through the town and arrived as planned at the harbour, where people had lined the whole harbour wall. Lachlan McKinnon had addressed the throng and given a well-received eulogy to Murdo McTavish and then led them in prayer for his soul before the final countdown to the New Year.

On the town clock's stroke of twelve Catriona Beamish stood in a spotlight on the harbour wall, her swimsuit and exposed body lathered in vegetable fat, and then did a stunning pencil dive into the dark harbour waters. Instantly, she resurfaced and started to swim powerfully across the moonlit water.

'Ladies and Gentlemen,' the Padre's voice boomed out from his loudhailer, 'we are sad to have lost our friend Murdo McTavish, but I give you the maid of Kyleshiffin, Murdo McTavish's great-niece, who just dived in and started to swim across the harbour, performing our age old tradition in the icy waters that herald in the New Year.'

Calum Steele took a swig of Glen Corlin single malt whisky from his hip flask and handed it to his friend, Torquil McKinnon. 'You'll be glad not to be pretending to be a maid and not having to swim in that icy cold water, Torquil, my man.'

'Aye, Calum, I'm glad that it is a real lassie that is taking the plunge. I've had enough of it myself.'

'And like the Padre said, Catriona Beamish is Skipper's relative. That's canny. A great choice.'

'Indeed, that was the unanimous opinion of the Hogmanay Dip and Nip committee. They'll be there to dry her off and give her a dram when she reaches the other side.'

He had not the slightest doubt that they would be there to pull her out and furnish her with a nip, just as he was sure that Murdo would have wanted Catriona to have his caul after all. And that was exactly what the whole Dip and Nip committee had agreed on. They all decided it was fitting.

As Torquil saw Catriona emerge from the water and climb the ladder to be helped onto the quay by the remaining band members, he felt a great relief and a warm glow. Catriona had done it, the islanders had paid their respects to Murdo, and the fine old West Uist tradition had been upheld.

He was suddenly aware of a female arm circling his waist. He turned to meet Lorna's lips.

'Happy Hogmanay, Inspector,' she whispered.

It was, to Torquil's mind, a Hogmanay to remember.

Want more adventures on the island of West Uist?
Start reading the Inspector Torquil McKinnon
Investigations series now!

Connect with Keith Moray!
Facebook/KeithMorayAuthor
Twitter: @KeithMorayTales
keithmorayauthor.com

THE SPIRIT OF CHRISTMAS BY CORA HARRISON

London, 1858

It was the week before Christmas. Queen Victoria had moved from Buckingham Palace to Sandringham for her Christmas celebrations, the Lord Mayor of London had held his Christmas dinner in Guildhall, toy shops were crowded with wonderful Christmas presents and an eleven-year-old orphan named Alfie was at his wits' end to find the increased rent before the end of the week, as well as to buy food and to get enough pieces of coal from the river to keep himself, his two cousins, his latest burden, little Olly, and above all his younger brother, blind Sammy, fed and warm in their damp, cold cellar.

Sammy couldn't remember a time when he could see the world around him. Alfie had told him that he had been blind since he was a baby. He had got a disease called measles and it made him blind, so their mother had said. He remembered his mother, but only vaguely. She had died from typhoid, from drinking dirty water from the pump nearby. He remembered his grandfather a little better. It was his grandfather who had taught him how to sing, and singing was the most important thing in his life.

And on this morning, two days before Christmas, Sammy took up his usual place in front of Hamley's toy shop in High Holborn and prepared to sing his heart out. Sammy knew what to do. He took in a deep breath, lifted his blind eyes towards the sky, felt the snowflakes fall upon his face and began to sing: 'Silent night, holy night; All is calm, all is bright...'

When he finished the carol, there was a few minutes' silence — he always loved that — and then a murmur of voices and lots of loud clapping. He heard Olly take the begging bowl around, heard the clink of the coins thrown into it, the stir of people moving on, as though released from a spell, and into the toy shop. Sammy felt himself glow with satisfaction.

And then everything went wrong.

Sammy heard a hoarse, rough voice. Olly squealed and protested. There was the sound of a blow. And then Mutsy, their faithful dog Mutsy, who Alfie had found at Smithfield and had trained to lead his blind brother through the streets of London, was barking savagely and growling.

Then there was a sudden, strong and slightly sweet smell. No more barking and no more growling. A thud on the pavement. The thud of a heavy body slumping on to the stone slabs.

Sammy instantly understood that he was without his protector. He stood very still, felt a blow on his own face and then moved off, stretching his hands in front of him, groping his way and trying to stop sobbing. The dog, dear Mutsy, had been dragged away. He had heard the sound of a heavy body slithering along the pavement. Had anyone noticed? He didn't know, but he knew that no one had interfered.

Someone had started singing a song about 'the spirit of Christmas' in a harsh, raucous voice and the air was full of drumbeats, loud and discordant. Sammy reached out a trembling hand, feeling for support, for a friendly arm, but could find nothing. The crowd had moved away; his acute senses told him that. Everyone had gone to listen to the man with the drum.

He was alone.

Sammy felt the cold sweat of fear break out. The icy air froze his skin and made him shiver inside his ragged clothing. He had never been alone before. Always there had been his brother Alfie holding his arm or else he had just reached over and curled his fingers around the leather collar on dear Mutsy's neck.

Hardly knowing what he was doing, Sammy stumbled away, both hands stretched out in front of him, desperately calling Mutsy's name.

The noise was bewildering. He had lived in London all of his life, so he was used to the sound of traffic, but now, without the support of a guiding hand, the uproar stunned and overwhelmed him: the rumbling of the iron wheels trundling over the cobbles, the iron shoes of the horses striking a rhythmic pattern in between and over above the rattle of the carts, the clank of the wheels, the shouts of the barrow boys, the street sellers, the organ grinders.

Sammy turned this way and that way, dizzy and befuddled. His path was blocked when he tried to get away from the sounds on the road, and the raucous, out-of-tune beat from the drum made him feel sick. Once more, he turned away from it and plunged in the opposite direction.

And then it seemed to him as though all hell had broken loose. A cacophony of horn blowing, yells, oaths, whinnying of horses and grinding of iron wheels against stone. In his despair, he had stumbled out onto the busiest street in London town. He turned to go back and then tripped and fell, hitting his sore cheek against the hard stone cobbles.

When Alfie turned up in High Holborn to collect his brother, Sammy, little Olly and the dog Mutsy, only Olly was to be seen. He stared incredulously at the man who had taken Sammy's place in front of William Hamley's toy shop, a placard around his neck with the words 'SPIRIT OF CHRISTMAS' printed upon it, a big fat man dressed in a fur-lined green robe, on his head a holly wreath set with shining icicles and in his hand a large cudgel with which he beat a drum to accompany his raucous singing. He had not just stolen the blind boy's begging place, but he had also taken Olly, whom Alfie fed and housed in order to look after Sammy.

Olly, with his half-starved appearance, his big frightened eyes and his ash-pale face, had proved a success. While Sammy sang Christmas carols in his beautiful voice, Olly took around the collecting bowl, coaxing pennies and even sixpences from the wealthy going to buy toys for their children's Christmas presents from Hamley's shop. But now Olly was using that same collecting bowl to get money for this strange man, and when Alfie tried to approach him, he had scuttled over to stand beside his new master.

Alfie eyed the cudgel in the man's hand and decided to keep his distance. Perhaps Sammy and Mutsy had gone home, turned away by rough words, or even a blow. He looked all around and then, on the other side of the road, he saw someone standing in the doorway of number 104 and waving to him. He knew the man. It was a Mr Lewis. He had the words 'Teacher of Shorthand' painted up on his window. And beside him was Sammy.

Alfie crossed the road with great care, the relief making his legs shake.

'They call him "Dirty Dan" in the pubs, or so I've heard,' said Mr Lewis with a nod in the direction of the large man.

Mr Lewis was kind. He had once shown Alfie how to write his name and the name of High Holborn in a few strange 'shorthand' symbols and then had given him an alphabet to practise writing secret messages. He sounded amused, now, but it was no joke for Alfie. This week before Christmas Day, outside Hamley's toy shop was the best place in London to touch the hearts of the rich. Year after year, Alfie had taken his blind brother to that spot and the pennies, four-penny and six-penny pieces all went into the rent box and kept him, his brother and his two cousins safely housed and fed for the month of January and sometimes February.

'What happened, Sam?' asked Alfie in a low voice, his hand on his brother's shoulder.

Sammy shrugged. 'He just pushed me away. Hit me.' There was a livid bruise on the blind boy's cheekbone.

'He was stumbling about on the edge of the road. A horse just avoided him. I came across to get him. Gave him a cup of hot chocolate and sat him by the fire, but he kept on wanting to be outside to wait for you,' said Mr Lewis.

'Mutsy? Where's Mutsy?' Alfie asked. Surely the big dog would have bitten anyone who hurt Sammy?

'Don't know,' said Sammy hopelessly. 'Just heard a voice saying, "Good dog, good dog" and then there was a funny smell! I think Mutsy fell. And then I got hit.'

Alfie clenched his hand so tightly that his nails dug into his palms. A funny smell. He had heard talk of this new stuff — chloroform, it was called. It had been used on shop workers during a raid in Tottenham Court Road. Chemists sold it and thieves and murderers bought it. Pour some onto a piece of cloth, shove it under someone's nose, and in two seconds, with no noise, it knocked out men — and dogs.

Mutsy was a large dog with a splendid pair of teeth that he kept sharp by killing rats at a phenomenal rate, and he would have defended Sammy until his last breath. He was probably dead by now, poor, faithful fellow, Alfie thought, blinking the tears from his eyes.

'And Olly? He took him, did he? I saw him.'

'Ollie didn't say a word,' said Sammy miserably. 'Didn't shout. Nothing. Heard him being dragged away.'

Alfie swore below his breath. Olly was useless. Why didn't he scream blue murder? But it was not surprising. He was no loss, but Mutsy... Alfie had a pain in his throat as if a large lump was choking him when he thought of the big loyal dog. He looked through the window at the man dressed as the 'Spirit of Christmas' and clenched his fists. But it was no good making a fuss. That would mean he'd end up thrown into gaol, and Sammy would have no means of finding his way home. Mutsy had always guided him everywhere.

'We'll try again tomorrow, Sam,' Alfie said as cheerfully as he could. 'Maybe the Peelers might move him on tonight.' The police, Alfie knew, did not like beggars, though they didn't usually bother a blind boy singing Christmas Carols. He just had to hope that the 'Spirit of Christmas' would be gone in the morning. They desperately needed the money. The landlord had already told him that the rent would go up in the New Year. If Sammy was prevented from singing outside Hamley's toy shop, then they might all end up sleeping on the street during the icy months of winter.

Alfie took his brother's hand. The tears were sliding down Sammy's pale face, but he could do nothing about that. The loss of Mutsy was a terrible tragedy, and no words could make it bearable at the moment.

Alfie slept very little that night, and he was awake when the church bells sounded the hour of six in the morning. It was a relief to get up and to get dressed, but he did it quietly. He would leave it to the last moment before he woke Sammy. First, he would fry some sausages to give his brother strength for the day ahead.

Alfie did his best to keep his mind away from Mutsy, but it was impossible. The dog was so much a part of their lives. He boiled some water, put some of it into a mug and added a teaspoon of honey from a jar given to him by a vicar who had admired Sammy's singing voice. And then he woke his brother, sprinkled some of the hot water on a rag and cleaned the blind boy's face. On another morning he might have washed his hair also, but this morning he didn't have the heart to bother. Chances were that all of this was useless.

'Breakfast, Sam,' Alfie said cheerfully and bit his lip as he saw how the blind boy automatically put out his hand as though to pat the dog which normally slept beside him. 'Wakey, wakey,' he said roughly to his cousins, Jack and Tom, and then handed Sammy a sausage wrapped in a piece of bread.

'Bit early, ain't it?' said Jack. 'It'd be black as midnight out there if t'weren't for the gas lamps.'

'Going to see if we can get the pitch early before that geezer nabs Sammy's place,' Alfie replied.

They would have a long cold wait for a couple of hours before the toy shop opened, he thought, but it couldn't be helped. High Holborn was a busy street, lined with shops: haberdashers and other clothiers, booksellers and stationers, silversmiths and jewellers, bullion sellers, food shops, organ shops, ironware, clock makers, gun sellers and locksmiths. They would get there about seven, he reckoned, but soon after eight in the morning it would be filled with men going to work. The important thing would be to lodge Sammy right in front of the door to Hamley's toy shop and to yell blue murder if that 'Spirit of Christmas' man tried to move them. It might work, he thought, forcing himself to be optimistic.

At least the place should be empty by the time that they arrived.

But it wasn't!

In front of the toy shop, there was a police van and a crowd of policemen going in and out of the bullion store beside the shop. Alfie didn't go any nearer. No point in annoying the police, he thought, but his sharp eyes could see that the lock on the front door to the bullion store had been cut out from the surrounding wood. He kept his hand on Sammy's shoulder and stood looking around him.

They were so early that the streetcleaners were still at work, heaping a cart with rubbish and filth, and some dead bodies. About usual at this time of the year. Alfie's eyes passed over the body of a well-dressed city gent with his face bashed in — a fight probably — and then a corpse of an old man, his rags and the crest of his bushy hair covered with frost. Frozen to death. Happened all the time. A dead bulldog, too, belonging to the bullion store, Alfie seemed to remember. And then he saw another body, half covered by the old man's. A small, naked leg and hand protruded from beneath the man's rags. He knew that hand, he thought.

'Stay here, Sammy, don't move!' he said and then went across the cart. 'Can I see that boy? Might be one of my brothers,' he added.

'You're no good to us unless you can take him away and get him buried yourself. Otherwise he gets tipped into the Crown Court burying ground with the rest of them.'

Alfie swallowed. He knew that burying ground, and he never wanted to go near it again for the rest of his life. 'Just want a quick look, and then I'll be on my way,' he said.

The man shrugged, but lifted a heavy stick and tipped the bundle of frozen rags and human flesh to one side. The dead man fell over with a thud. Yes, it was Olly beneath him, but there was something odd about his head, twisted to one side, resting on his shoulder.

'Neck broken,' said the streetcleaner. 'Found him like that. Someone broke it, before he froze.' He shrugged his shoulders. 'Well, d'you want him?'

Alfie shook his head. 'Naw, nothing to do with me. Come on, Sammy.' He was deeply uneasy, though. These streetcleaners knew their business, and during the winter months they collected bodies from the streets every morning. 'Someone broke his neck,' the man had said. Why would anyone break Olly's neck?

Alfie moved away, back towards the toy shop. He needed to find out what was going on. Tentatively, he approached the space in front of the bullion store and patted one of the lively-looking police horses champing at the bit.

'Nice horse,' he said to a young policeman standing nearby. He jerked his head towards the door with the missing lock. 'Holy Mackerel,' he said. 'Don't tell me that all them bars of gold in the place been stolen.'

The man just gave a sidelong glance at the sergeant, and Alfie went back to Sammy. There was no sense in allowing his brother to stand around shivering and letting the cold air spoil his voice. Hamley's toy shop opened at nine o'clock. It wouldn't be worthwhile for his brother to start singing for another few hours. He himself could hold the place for Sammy in the teeth of the 'Spirit of Christmas' man while the police were around to protect him. But what could he do with Sammy?

Then across the road a door opened, and Mr Lewis appeared in his dressing gown. He wanted to see what had happened, no doubt. Alfie did not hesitate. Rapidly he grabbed his brother's arm and steered him across the wide road as quickly as he could go.

'Morning, Mr Lewis,' he called, getting the greeting out before he reached the pavement in case the man might disappear indoors out of the cold. 'Been a robbery, Mr Lewis. Millions of gold bars stolen.'

'My word, that's exciting,' said Mr Lewis. He looked across the road and then down at his slippers and dressing gown. 'I'd better get dressed.'

'I'll go back and find out everything for you,' said Alfie eagerly. 'Could my brother wait in your hall until I come back? Don't want the cold to get into his throat.'

'Come on, Sammy.' Mr Lewis put out a hand and took Sammy's arm. 'Let's go in and drink some of that hot chocolate that you liked so much. We'll have a mug ready for you, too, Alfie, so don't be long.'

Alfie was crossing over the road again almost before the man finished speaking. He turned his mind firmly away from Olly's death and focused on the future. This was working out well. The police would be there for most of the day, he reckoned. He'd have a chat with them about Sammy. Mention something about Olly if he needed to.

He gave a quick look around when he reached the other side of the road. To his disappointment, most of the police were piling into the van — going back for their breakfast, perhaps. A sergeant was left talking to the ironmonger from number 54, Joseph Nettleford, brought along to fix the door lock, guessed

Alfie, and a bored-looking policeman marched up and down the pavement.

Alfie edged a little closer to the sergeant while pretending to search the pavement for a dropped coin.

'I just don't understand it,' the ironmonger was saying. 'That lock on the trapdoor is perfect. Not been touched. I'd have been surprised if anything could have drilled through that steel, not without making the most tremendous racket. The cellar itself is like a giant safe with a steel door, you know. That was my idea. The clerk goes up and down on a ladder. And he has that little "dumb waiter" lift to shift the bars of bullion in case he breaks his neck carrying these heavy loads of gold bullion up and down a ladder. As for the front door lock, well, that was done from the inside.

'It was the clerk; I'm sure of that. You tell me he's missing. Well, he's the one that has stolen your bullion bars. And that would explain how the policeman on duty in the street heard the dog bark during the night. The clerk loosed the bulldog every night and left him locked in the building. No thief would have dared face him. He's a killer, they say. The clerk was the only one who could touch him. He was the one who fed the brute.'

'Well, there's a hue and cry out after him now,' said the sergeant. 'So that's what they have a dumb waiter lift for? I wondered about that. Wondered if it might have been a restaurant once. They use them for sending dishes up from the kitchen in a place that I go to for my dinner, though a much bigger one than that little one in there.'

Alfie listened and frowned. A germ of an idea had come to him. He gave a hasty glance at the policeman deep in talk with the locksmith and then slipped silently on his bare feet through the doorway and into the bullion store.

It was not what he expected, he thought. He had imagined it like Aladdin's Cave — he had read a story about that in school — had thought that there would be shelves lined with gold bars, but the room was empty of everything except one desk, the very small lift, wide open, showing one empty shelf within it, a ladder hanging from the wall, and in the middle of the floor a large square of steel with a complicated lock on one side of it.

A locked trapdoor. That's what the locksmith had been talking about.

But then he heard something. A muted howl. He knew that sound and made straight for the back door. There was a key in it. Alfie opened it quickly. He saw an empty yard and a dog kennel. There had been a dog always in it. Alfie had heard him bark every day that they had spent in High Holborn. A vicious beast, someone had told him once, but now he knew that the vicious beast was no more. He had seen the bulldog's dead body slung into the cart that cleared the rubbish from the street.

This lonely wail did not come from that bulldog. Alfie knew the sound. It was Mutsy.

And there he was. Mutsy, an oozing wound on his forehead and his nose and mouth encased in a muzzle. Alfie took one eager step forward, and then a hand clamped over his nose and mouth, a rough cloth, a strong, sweet smell.

Alfie struggled frantically, scratching the hand and kicking, but his strength was ebbing fast.

Nothing could save him now. Mutsy was locked into the kennel with a vicious muzzle clamping his jaws. Alfie's body and the body of his faithful dog would be on that cart early next morning and would be thrown on to the festering piles in the burying ground.

Alfie woke to a hot breath on his face. And then there was a familiar voice. The voice of a kind police inspector who had helped Alfie out in the past.

'Well, there you are, Alfie. Back to us again. I've got a nice sharp knife if you want to get that muzzle off your dog. I thought that I'd wait for you to do it, though I know he's a good-tempered fellow.'

When Alfie had released Mutsy, he sat for a long minute with his face buried in the dog's fur and then he gathered up his strength, took the knife and sawed through the leather strap. 'I was going to come and see you, Inspector Denham,' he said and heard that his voice sounded strange and wavering even to his own ears.

'Yes, you should have. I'd have got the sergeant to release Mutsy. You'd have done that, sergeant, wouldn't you?'

'Sir,' said the sergeant in a doubtful tone of voice.

Alfie shook his head violently, trying to clear his brains. 'No, not that. Not about Mutsy. I thought Mutsy was dead...'

'Get a cup of tea for the boy, sergeant. Take your time, Alfie.'

By the time that the policeman came back with a steaming mug, saying, 'Fellow in the toy shop made us a pot,' Alfie was himself again. It was the first time that he had ever tasted tea. He didn't like the taste, would have preferred beer, but he gulped it down and it helped to clear his head a little.

'No, not Mutsy,' he repeated. 'This robbery. I knows how they done it.'

He stroked Mutsy for a moment, willing the strength back into his legs, and then got to his feet and led the way back into the bullion store.

'It's the dumb waiter,' he said and stopped opposite the small square opening with its wooden platform suspended by ropes.

'You pull it up and down like this,' he said. 'Pull these two ropes, Inspector, and it goes down to the cellar, and pull the other two and it comes up.' His head was clear now and he looked triumphantly at the inspector, who looked back at him with a puzzled frown.

'That's right,' said the sergeant. 'They use it to send the bullion down to the cellar, sir. The man sends down the dumb waiter to the cellar, unlocks the trapdoor and then goes down to the cellar via the ladder. He takes the bullion off the shelves down there — it's like a giant safe down there, sir, all lined with steel and the trapdoor is like a safe door — and if he needs any bullion, he goes down, locks the trapdoor behind him, loads the dumb waiter with the gold bars, climbs back up, locks the trapdoor, probably locks the front door too before he hauls up the dumb waiter and gives the customer his gold.'

'And that's how they did the robbery,' said Alfie triumphantly. 'Naught to do with the clerk — you'll find his dead body in the Crown Court burying ground. I see'd him in the cart yesterday morning. Sawed the front door lock while he was out at lunch; killed him when he came back. That's why they wanted the man banging that drum. Stopped anyone hearing the noise. Someone planned it out really well. Got rid of Sammy and put that "Spirit of Christmas" man in his place and told him to bang away at the drum, stole our dog so that the barking would be heard at night and everyone would blame the clerk.'

Alfie smiled to himself as he saw the puzzled expression on the face of the clever Scotland Yard Inspector. Still, he could explain everything afterwards. Now he had to show the real cleverness of the plot.

'So no one opened the trapdoor lock to the cellar,' Alfie said quietly. 'They knew they couldn't do that. They just sent someone down in the dumb waiter. He loaded all the gold onto it and they pulled him up again. Never touched that trapdoor lock.'

'Him?' said the inspector. 'Good God, Alfie, you couldn't put a man on that dumb waiter. It wouldn't take anything much bigger than a small dog.'

'Not a man, a little boy, a very little boy,' said Alfie and heard a note of sadness in his own voice. 'They stole little Olly that took around the begging bowl for Sammy when he was singing. He were ever so tiny. Brought up on a Baby Farm, and they teach them to manage on very small rations in them places, sir. He'd have fitted on that shelf and left plenty of room for the gold. Wouldn't have weighed much neither.'

'Where's the boy now?' The Inspector jumped up from his seat on the desk.

'In the burying ground,' said Alfie grimly. 'And his neck was broken before he was put there, just to make him nice and tidy-like. You'd better get your men after a geezer who dresses up as the "Spirit of Christmas". He's known as "Dirty Dan" in the pubs, so I've heard. He's the one that chloroformed me. He mightn't be far away. I'll be off now, Inspector. Thanks for the tea, Sergeant.'

Alfie busied himself with stroking Mutsy to give the inspector a chance to put his hand in his pocket and slip a coin to him.

A florin, no less, Alfie thought with satisfaction as he crossed the road towards Mr Lewis's house. A florin would keep the rent collector at bay for the foreseeable future. Now he would just have to collect Sammy. Mr Lewis had seen him from the window and had the door open.

'Come in, Alfie, and bring Mutsy too. I'm glad to see him. Go in there by the fire with Sammy while I make some fresh chocolate. Here they are, Sammy.'

Alfie smiled slightly at the sight of Sammy and Mutsy's reunion. He bent down to pick up a piece of paper that had fallen out of a notebook on a small table, knocked over by Mutsy in his rush towards Sammy. Shorthand, he thought and settled down to see if he could read some of it. And then his eye was caught by a pair of words which seemed to come up again and again on the page of writing.

'DUMB WAITER', he translated. He made out another few words and then replaced the page as though it burned his hand. He made up his mind instantly, as Mr Lewis brought in a tray of three steaming hot chocolate-filled mugs and a plateful of biscuits. He even produced a beef shinbone from his pocket for Mutsy.

Olly's death may not have been planned, Alfie told himself firmly. And Mutsy would probably have been released at the end of the day. And no one had harmed Sammy.

And, anyway, who was he to do the policemen's job for them?

'You're very kind to us, sir,' Alfie said as he sipped his hot chocolate and looked across at his brother, safe and well with his hand on the neck of their beloved dog.

Want to solve more mysteries with Alfie and the gang?
Start reading the Victorian London Murder Mysteries
series now!

Connect with Cora Harrison!
www.coraharrison.com

THE STOLEN SANTA SACK BY SEÁN GIBBONS

Galway, Ireland, 2019

It could be said that everything that happens is good news for somebody. How driving along a motorway, at two o'clock in the morning shortly before Christmas, with a dead Santa Claus in the back of his cab could ever be good news for Ben Miller was anybody's guess.

He'd been hired by Superintendent Martin Folan to do no more than collect this edition of the white-bearded man from the most exclusive hotel in Galway and deposit him at an address in Athenry, a journey of less than 25kms. Heck, hadn't the Superintendent himself even come out to the front of the hotel to pay him? The Superintendent had helped Santa into the taxi and handed him a big sack that surely, on reflection, should have been empty rather than bursting at the seams. Miller, at the time counting the notes Superintendent Folan had thrust into his hand, had dismissed this as an unimportant detail.

The sack's absence, when Miller pulled up on the hard shoulder and went back to check on his passenger, who had just toppled over on the back seat, suggested problems with his analysis. *I'm really on top of my game tonight*, Miller thought, when he spotted the handle of a dagger sticking out of the old guy's chest, right where the heart ought to be doing its thing. There was no obvious reason to check for a pulse, but he did so anyway. Just in case anyone asked him later.

His mobile rang. A sound no one welcomed in the middle of the night. Especially if you were Ben Miller and the name 'Folan' was lighting up the screen.

'Where are you?' the little cop said, panic in his tone.

'On my way back into town,' Miller said. He had remembered hearing something going on in his cab after he had picked Santa up, sometime around the time he had been stuck at the roadworks at the top of Eyre Square in Galway. He'd put it down to his rather muffin-shaped passenger's need to expel a bit of trapped wind. You got used to all kinds of goings-on in the back of your car when you drove a taxi for a living.

There was no sign of damage to the car, so either the rear window had been rolled down or the rear passenger door had been opened. The old guy must have known his killer.

'Well, get back here straight away,' Folan was saying. 'Have you still got that fecker with you?'

'In a manner of speaking.'

Folan mustn't have heard him properly. 'Well, don't let him get away from you.' *Bit late for that*, thought Miller. 'You bring him straight to me. I'm still at the hotel.'

The hotel staff were busy trying to rid themselves of the last of the revellers. A group of men and women descended on Miller's cab. No notice was taken of the dead passenger. The most inebriated of them, as usual, tried to negotiate passage. Miller ran an eye over them — a couple of women who looked like they might leave a deposit on the upholstery made his decision easy.

'He's already booked.' Folan elbowed them out of the way; not an easy thing for a man no taller than your average elf to do. 'Christ!' he added when he spotted the recently deceased

Santa. The Superintendent was sporting a tuxedo that made him look like demented bauble.

'Santa, actually,' said Miller. 'The other guy's cornered Easter.'

'Get this heap of junk out of here,' Folan said, not in any mood for spoofing. 'Bring it up round the side of the building. I'll be out to you in a minute. And don't let anybody see him.'

The side of the hotel was dark. A pair of human rats scampered off into the night when the taxi, all lit up like it was still for hire, appeared.

'Rudolph and the boys will be wondering where you are,' Miller said to the corpse who, he could now see, had been spilling blood like it was going out of fashion. The leather upholstery was proving its worth once again.

Miller felt the body. It was cold. The blood was already dry.

'What did you do to him?' Folan said when he reappeared. 'I always said your driving would be the death of someone.' He'd draped his expensive overcoat over his shoulders. He reminded Miller of Edward G. Robinson in some long-forgotten film. 'The boys are on their way,' he added. Folan shoved Miller aside and stuck his head into the rear of the car. 'Where's the sack?' he said.

'I couldn't tell you,' Miller said. 'He had it and then he didn't have it. You know what they say about not being able to take it with you.'

'You're not a funny guy,' Folan said. 'And, even if you were, I'm in no mood for jokes. Or stupidity.'

Their repartee was interrupted by the arrival of 'Defective' Sergeant Brady and Detective Gárda Peadar Wallace.

'What's up, boss?' Brady said.

'Take a look for yourself,' Folan said.

The DS eased his massive frame through the rear passenger door of the cab.

'Be careful,' said Miller. 'Don't push the frame out of line.'

'Jesus,' said Brady. 'They've got Santa.'

'Don't worry,' Miller said to Wallace, who was looming over Brady like a crane. 'It's not the real one.'

'For the last time, Miller,' Folan screeched, 'shut the fuck up!'

'Where's the sack?' Brady's voice sounded like it was coming from inside the dead body.

'That's what I've been trying to get this idiot to tell me,' Folan said.

'Do you want us to jog his memory a bit?' Wallace said. The cop had long had it in for Miller and would relish an opportunity to renew the taxi-driver's acquaintanceship with his fists.

'Leave it for a bit,' the Superintendent said. He turned to Miller and held him in his gaze. 'I'm going to ask you nicely for now,' he said, 'where's the sack your man had with him when he got into this heap of crap?'

'And I'm going to tell you just as nicely,' Miller said. 'I don't know. One minute the guy's as alive as you are; the next minute he's as dead as a doornail and the sack's gone.' Miller fixed his eyes on those of Folan. 'No more than that do I know.'

'But you must have a theory or two,' Folan said.

'You overestimate my intelligence,' Miller said.

'Don't make the mistake of overestimating my patience,' Folan said.

'I thought I heard a bit of a kerfuffle in the back seat,' Miller said, 'when we were held up at the roadworks on Richardson's corner. I put it down to your man farting, but now it makes sense because Santa's dead, his sack is gone and there's no damage to my car, which can only mean he knew whoever it was who took his sack.'

'It wasn't his sack,' said Folan.

'No, it belonged to the Super,' said Brady, an admission of fact that brought him a long steely stare from his boss.

'Gobshite,' said Folan. 'Anyway, Miller, now you have it. The sack is mine and what's in it is mine and I want it back. And I want you to get it back for me.'

'Jesus,' said Miller, 'didn't your dear old mammy ever tell you not to be so greedy?'

'I need that sack back by noon tomorrow,' Folan said.

Less than twenty-four hours.

'What do I do with Santa?' Miller said.

'You can stuff him down a chimney for all I care,' Folan said.

Folan wasn't the type to indulge in confidences, but there was something about tonight's situation that rendered him loose-tongued. He shooed his colleagues away and, rather unnecessarily, ushered Miller into an even darker corner than the one they'd been occupying. His nervousness expressed itself in a series of farts that left Miller gasping for fresh air. Folan checked the time on his phone, the light from which reflected off the sheen of sweat covering his porcine face.

'You know about the dinner dance?' he began. 'The one that was on in the hotel here tonight?'

Miller didn't feel that merited a response.

'Well,' continued the Superintendent. 'Your man — Santa that is — was doing more than just giving out Christmas presents; he was also receiving them, and he was supposed to hand them up at the end of the night. Only he didn't. The fucker gave me an empty sack and made off with the full one. I didn't spot it until after you'd gone off with him. I tried to get those two idiots over there to go after you, but they were already on a call…'

'Proper police business, you mean?' Miller said. Though he couldn't see it, he could sense Folan's fist form a ball that, if he wasn't careful, would connect with his own more delicate orbs. He took an involuntary step backwards.

'I'm only going to tell you once more, Miller,' Folan said, 'don't piss me off tonight.' He let that hang for a pregnant moment. 'The sack contained donations to various, er, charitable causes that it was my sworn duty to hand over to their rightful recipients.' The Super hadn't a charitable thought in his repertoire. 'And now I can't do that thanks to that prick.' The cop's bad breath drifted in the air between them. 'I was meant to make the handover tomorrow evening, so you've got about sixteen hours to recover the missing item.'

'Hey,' said Miller. 'This has nothing to do with me. I did all I was supposed to do. Now, I just want to get back to work. I'm losing money here by the minute.'

'You call that pittance you make money? There was more money in that sack than the likes of you will see in a dozen lifetimes. And I want it back. And you're going to get it back for me. And Brady and Wallace are going to be watching your every move.'

'Is there anything else you can tell me?' Miller said eventually.

'There's been a bit of rumbling,' Folan said after some thought, 'that a certain Mr Chin would like to acquire a rather lucrative enterprise with which I am associated.' He gave him the address of a Chinese takeaway in the Newcastle area of the city that everyone knew was no more than a front for an illegal gambling den.

This was more than just a schoolyard quarrel.

'What do I do with our friend in the back of my cab?' Miller said.

'I've already told you, I don't care.'

The Superintendent emitted a final fart and disappeared into the night.

Disposing of a body is not as easy as it might seem, especially when the body is that of a man known to you and the entire world by well-honed reputation. The Santa in the back of Miller's cab had started to shed white, hair-like strands from his beard, red hat and cuffed sleeves. Miller nabbed Brady and Wallace just before they managed to slink off into the night.

'I'm shooting myself in the foot here,' Miller said, 'but didn't your Super tell you to keep an eye on me?'

They may have exchanged confirmation-seeking looks. They may even have nodded in agreement, but it was too dark for Miller to see any of this.

'Well?' he said.

'He did —' DS Brady was the spokesman — 'but since you're probably heading off for a bit of shut-eye, we thought we might do the same.'

'You're hardly going to need watching while you're asleep, are you?' Wallace contributed.

'Aren't you forgetting something?' Miller said.

Silence.

'Santa Claus,' Miller prompted. 'And more importantly, getting rid of the body. You don't want me going around with him like that in the back of my cab, do you? Telling everybody he belongs to your boss.'

That got them moving.

'What are you going to do with him?' Brady said. 'Any ideas?'

Miller wasn't surprised that he'd been nominated as the brains of the operation. He'd been thinking about it. 'Come on,' he said. 'In you get.'

DS Brady took the front passenger seat; his bulk spilled out over the gear stick, and it caused the left hand side of the car to genuflect slightly. Wallace sat beside the corpse.

The takeaway Folan had mentioned had shut up shop for the night. At least the sale of dubious curries had ceased. However, a steady trickle of men continued to scurry in and out through the narrow door to the side of the premises. Every time someone approached the door from the streetside, it was illuminated by a sensor-activated security light. Miller had parked on the opposite side of the street. It soon became clear that every ten minutes or so a heavy-set man stuck his head out through this door and scanned the surrounding area. Places like this stayed open all night, so it meant they had only a ten-minute window to do what Miller had in mind.

He explained his plan to the two cops. Then all three of them lifted Santa out of the car and put him down on the pavement. Ten minutes expired during the course of this phase of the operation.

They hoisted Santa's corpse; rigor mortis had set in and the body, which they'd dumped unceremoniously on the ground, had assumed an unwieldy shape that was awkward to manhandle. They were all guilty of dropping him at least once during the brief journey to the other side of the road.

Miller directed them towards the side entrance, thankfully much underused in the intervening period. The cops could move surprisingly fast when they wanted to, and they soon had the body propped up against the door, which Miller had ascertained opened outwards.

Someone tried to open the door from the inside. They tried again, harder this time, upon meeting the resistance provided by the body. A perforated conversation told them help had been enlisted. A more determined, but equally futile, effort to shove the door open followed. Miller thought it was time they got out of there.

They'd parked the car in the lee of a row of houses that had thankfully provided an arched alleyway down which they could run into concealment. Neither of the cops seemed to have had much experience of this aspect of their calling; Miller had been ducking and diving since his childhood. He had trouble getting them to keep their heads down and was only grateful that he had been able to stop them from putting on their hi-vis jackets. Gárda Wallace was still muttering something about safety and unions when the heavy-set gentleman left the takeaway though the door normally used by hungry customers and approached the body blocking the other entrance.

'Who's that?' he said to a second man who had followed him into the open. They scratched their heads vigorously, as if trying to rustle up recognition.

In the meantime, a trio of punters had arrived, looking to gain access to the illegal casino. The heavy-set man's companion ushered them through the takeaway door and returned to assist with the removal of the body. Before laying hands on Santa's corpse, they took a good look round and then, with great difficulty, lifted the dead man off the ground and half-carried half-dragged him to the pharmacist's premises next door. There they deposited him by the front door.

'Now,' said Miller. 'That's how you shift the blame.'

'What do we do now?' DS Brady said.

'What you do now is tell me what you know about this place,' Miller said. 'And don't go all dumb on me because, judging from your lack of wide-eyed wonder, I know it's not news to you. You've been here with the Super, haven't you?'

The cops exchanged looks.

'I won't tell if you don't,' Miller said.

'Let me at him, Sarge,' Wallace said. Brady looked like he would like nothing better.

'No,' the DS said. 'There'll be plenty of time for that later, but we need to make sure things are sorted out properly for the boss first.'

They had retreated further down the alley and were in a little yard surrounded by grubby, dimly lit flats that hinted of somnolent residents. They were probably used to all manner of nocturnal goings-on outside their doors and were wise enough to pay them no heed.

'Alright,' DS Brady assumed the role of spokesman. 'The Super knows all about Mr Chin's operation and takes a cut for turning the other way.' No surprises there. But Brady wasn't finished yet. 'He's also part of a syndicate that places really big bets every now and then…'

'We're all part of it,' Wallace interrupted.

'And these bets are placed on football matches or horse races that are fixed,' Miller said.

Brady's clenched jowls were confirmation enough.

'And tonight's bets were placed under the guise of charitable donations dropped into Santa's sack?'

Brady's jowls unclenched long enough to spur Miller on.

'Only Santa double-crossed Folan and left him holding an empty sack, which doesn't bode well for his position amongst the remainder of the syndicate, apart from you two Spaniels, that is.'

Wallace growled in the background.

'Then Santa was double-crossed and killed in his turn.' Miller needed a smoke. He sparked up and inhaled deeply. 'So who the hell was Santa when he was at home?'

Wallace waited for Brady to offer enlightenment. The DS squirmed. 'Charlie Coughlan,' he said at last. 'He used to be in the Force, but he was retired early a few years back.' That meant he'd been a bold boy, bold enough to have done something counter-cultural in a police service renowned for its ability to close ranks and stick together.

'What did he do?' said Miller. 'Steal the tea money?'

'He nearly broke the Credit Union,' said Wallace. Clearly he had been personally affected by Coughlan's perfidy.

'So what was the Santa gig all about?' Miller said.

'It was the Super's way of getting him to pay back some of what he owed us,' Brady said.

Only Charlie Claus may have had other debts that Folan hadn't known about, and handing over a sack stuffed with cash was meant to clear them. But in that case, why kill him? And why in my fucking cab, thought Miller. It would be interesting too to know for whom the sack had been ultimately destined.

Anyway, Superintendent Folan had been double-crossed and he was mad as hell about that; Santa had also had the dirt done on him and he was getting set to fertilise the daisies. It seemed imperative to Miller that they find whoever it was Santa's sack was meant to end up with, for they would surely know the identities of his killers.

'Something's happening,' Wallace called from the opening of the alley, where he'd taken up sentry duty.

Sure enough, a red Mercedes-Benz W123 had just pulled up outside the curry house. Only one man in Galway still drove such a car — Columbanus Chin, an old acquaintance of Miller's. As his surname suggested, Mr Chin was Chinese; as his forename suggested, he had a sense of the surreal. He'd once told Miller he'd adopted the name 'Columbanus' because it made him sound like he might have roots in "the sacred soil of Hibernia". He'd laughed at his grasp of tourist board marketing lingo. Miller had found his laughter contagious.

Now here Mr Chin was, on a freezing cold night shortly before Christmas, pulled out of his warm bed to bend over the body of Santa Claus. Mr Chin was quite simply the tiniest man Miller had ever encountered in all his almost fifty years. He reminded Miller of a child playing dress-up in his father's best suit. What he lacked in physical stature was more than compensated for by his reputation as a hard-nosed businessman, albeit one whose wisely-invested wealth came from unorthodox sources. In the early days, shortly after his unheralded arrival in Galway, he'd made regular use of Miller's services until he acquired a vehicle of his own. The Merc he was driving was just the latest in a long line.

Even Brady and Wallace seemed to know who Mr Chin was; and they looked like they'd much rather not have known. Miller couldn't blame them there.

The miniature man poked at the corpse with a pointy-toed shoe and almost immediately bent down to wipe it clean again.

'You'd think he'd have somebody to do that for him by now, wouldn't you?' Miller said.

The cops grunted.

'I guess that rules out either of you ever applying for the job then,' Miller continued. He could sense his companions' fists take form.

'How did he get here?' Mr Chin said to the heavy-set man, who merely shrugged his shoulders. 'Where is the sack?' Mr Chin continued. His aide added a look of puzzlement to his shrug.

'What do we do with him?' the heavy-set man asked, but Mr Chin was already talking on his mobile and didn't answer the question.

'I bet,' said Miller, 'that he's on to your boss. And, if you're game, I can give you very good odds on what's going to happen next.'

Brady and Wallace shared incredulous looks.

'What?' Miller said. 'No takers? I'd have put both you boys down as the type who likes a safe bet.' His mobile phone shrilled. 'You see — can't say I didn't tell you.' He winked at them. 'Superintendent Folan, how are you?'

Brady and Wallace stood almost to attention.

'What the fuck are you at?' Folan said.

'I'm not at anything,' Miller said. 'Apart, that is, from watching your miniature poodle scratching his head. You told me to leave Santa's body here. I've done what you told me to do, and mine is not to reason why. In other words, I don't know what point you're trying to make to Mr Chin, but I don't think he's getting it.'

Folan merely harrumphed.

'I think,' Miller said, 'that you need to tell me what possessed you to trust Charlie Coughlan with all that dosh. Haven't gone soft in your old age, have you?' Unless, Miller thought, it was all part of some overriding scheme of the Superintendent's. Nothing was beyond Folan.

'Miller,' Folan said. 'I'm not paying you to think…'

'Apart from dropping Santa back to the North Pole,' Miller said, 'you have never paid me to do anything. I'm on my own time, and I can think all I want. And I think I know what's going on. In fact, I take my hat off to you. But you're still left with a pair of problems.'

One of those 'problems', Mr Chin, was, at that very minute, scratching his head vigorously. He and his bodyguard were standing outside the takeaway, seemingly examining the menu stuck to the window, as if it would provide some of the answers the little Chinese man was seeking.

The other in that pair of problems, the corpse of Santa Claus, was proving to be a distraction to the area's feline population, a ginger member of which was playing with the man's white beard, which now looked like it might actually be real.

'I'm not a gambling man,' said Miller, 'but I bet that, if I was, I could safely wager my life savings on Kevin Sherlock's involvement somewhere along the line. I have heard talk about his recent move onto Mr Chin's turf … and, no, don't pardon the pun.'

Kevin Sherlock was a well-known drug dealer with whom Miller had history. Superintendent Folan used Sherlock's lack of knowledge about the full nature of this history to keep Miller in line.

'Well,' Folan said at last. 'I don't think you really want to go there, do you?'

Miller didn't need to confirm that the cop was right, but in for a penny in for a pound. 'I think,' he said, 'that you're setting Columbanus Chin and Kevin Sherlock up against one another with the aim of scooping up the fallout. Smart move there, Superintendent. Was putting an end to Christmas part of the plan?'

'What are you on about now?' Folan said.

'Santa's dead — in case you've forgotten. How are you going to explain that one to the millions of kids all over the world expecting the man in red to come down their chimneys in a couple of nights?'

'Get that body out of there!'

'Supposing you tell me first what's going on. Why did Santa Claus double-cross you? And who killed him?'

'I reckon he had debts of his own, and he was planning to use our little collection to clear them. Only he decided to mess with Sherlock.'

'So you're saying Sherlock had him killed?'

'He's not someone who likes to be taken for a patsy.'

'You don't say!'

'Get rid of that body is what I do say.' Folan hung up.

Miller turned to Brady and Wallace. 'I don't know how much of that you managed to overhear, but the Super wants you to get rid of the body.'

'How are we supposed to do that?' DS Brady said.

All three of them were examining the lie of the land. Dawn was approaching, but at least Mr Chin had taken his leave. The bodyguard wasn't as busy with his door-keeping duties, as only the insomniac gamblers were on the loose at that hour, so there were more opportunities for them to nip across the road and retrieve the body.

'What do we do with him now?' Wallace said when they'd carried Santa across the road and deposited him in the alley. 'We can't call the barracks at this hour.'

'No,' Brady said. 'The Super'll go mad if we involve anybody else.'

'You could just leave him here. Let some other sucker find him, and then it's over to your boss to ensure the investigation turns out to be inconclusive,' Miller suggested.

The cops looked at one another. How long would it take them to realise what a neatly packaged proposal they'd just been presented with? Not long, as it turned out.

'Any chance of a lift back to the barracks?' Brady said.

'Take a taxi — there should be one along any minute.'

Now, there's one Santa who won't be trailing sooty boots all over Mother's nice clean carpet any time soon. The only question remaining was: would Christmas be saved?

Nothing to do with me, Miller consoled himself as he drove away.

Keep an eye out for the Ben Miller Thriller Series, coming soon!

Connect with Seán Gibbons!
Twitter: @SeanGibbons58

WILL POWER BY MARILYN TODD

London, 1895

'No, no, no, and just to be clear, no. You are not coming inside.'

That's the trouble with cats. It's not that they don't understand English. It's the obeying orders part where they tend to have problems. Before Julia McAllister had even finished, a flash of lithe tabby shot past her skirts faster than lightning buttered both sides. Wishful thinking said it was the lure of a blazing log fire on this cold, wintery morning. Reality put its money on the joint of boiled gammon that sat in the kitchen, covered only loosely by a tea-towel.

Julia set her equipment down on the pavement, not easy in her ridiculous wasp-waist corsets, and weighed up her choices. Either spend the next ten minutes trying to round up this slippery little eel — twenty, if the wretched thing dived into her studio and hid among the props — or be late for her appointment at the undertaker's, where Mr. Palmer was waiting for her to take a photo of his wife in her coffin. The only portrait he would ever have of her.

Hearing a noise that sounded suspiciously like the grinding of her own teeth, Julia locked the door, picked up her camera, tucked her tripod under her arm and set a brisk pace down the street.

The widower, dishevelled, unshaven, haggard and drawn, shook her hand. But only out of politeness.

'Mind telling me what Whitmore deems so desperately important, that he sends his assistant?' he asked.

What could she say? That Sam Whitmore had died four years ago? That he'd left his business to the waif he'd rescued, thereby forcing Julia to pretend that he was still in charge and add a "Mrs" to her name, simply because politicians thought women's brains weren't the equal of a man's?

'Your wife died unexpectedly in childbirth,' Julia said gently. 'With such a grievous double loss, Mr. Whitmore felt it more sensitive for a woman to take her portrait.' She laid a hand on his crumpled sleeve. 'He wouldn't entrust me with the job, if he didn't think I was up to it.'

'Of course, of course, I'm sorry, that was rude…'

Leaving the distraught widower in the care of the undertaker, Julia slipped into the chapel of rest and set to work with her cosmetics and comb, because, let's face it, Julia thought, every girl wants to look her best for a portrait.

'Not fair, is it?' she whispered, applying rouge to Mrs. Palmer's cold cheeks. 'Your husband ought to be dragging a tree back to the house right now. Standing on a kitchen chair, strapping the angel on the top and placing candles in the branches while you hang sparkly baubles to celebrate Baby's First Christmas together.'

Instead, the only church service Mrs. Palmer would be attending was her funeral, and even then, Julia thought, fluffing the dead girl's leg o' mutton sleeves to their fullest, she'd be alone. Stillborn, and therefore not baptised, Baby Palmer didn't qualify for Christian burial.

An hour later, with the widower's grief clinging like a tick, but at least a decent batch of glass plates to work from and give him comfort, Julia was back outside her studio.

'Well, now! You're the last thing I expected.'

Clearly, the little tabby had also weighed up the odds before she left, deciding that outside-and-free beat being banged-up-inside. Julia set down her tripod, about to dig out her key, when she suddenly stopped.

The cat hadn't rushed out when she'd turned to lock up. The door was jemmied open.

She looked up and down the street. It was busy at the best of times, never mind with everyone bundled up in mufflers and scarves, caps pulled low, heads to the ground, rushing about posting cards, buying presents, stocking up on everything from nuts to oranges to crackers in a windchill which stopped even polar bears from hanging round for the sake of it.

Julia sighed, then did the only thing possible under the circumstances. She cocked her British Bulldog revolver and ventured inside.

Barely fifteen minutes later, as the bells of St. Oswald's chimed the half-hour, it was clear that the thief was not only long gone, but that he hadn't broken in for the cash. The money was still in the till, every last farthing, and he hadn't tossed the place for jewellery or stolen a single silver photo frame from the display. In fact, every room from her bedroom to the scullery remained untouched, except for the ham, which had been pulled off the plate and gnawed round the edges, though somehow she didn't think that was the thief's doing. No, the only room he'd ransacked was her studio, and despite the stack of saucy photographs that financed Julia's independence, all that was missing were prints of the Kents' wedding last Saturday.

And sod's law, Mrs. Kent was due round any second to pick out the best ones and choose frames.

'Everyone said it was bad luck to marry in December.'

Far from being agitated, angry, flustered or accusing — all of which Julia was braced for — the new wife merely shrugged. Mind you, Mrs. Kent didn't exactly fit the stereotype of the blushing bride in any form or type. Indifferent had been the word that kept running through Julia's head while arranging group shots in the churchyard. Mrs. Kent had been unconcerned about who stood where, what mischief the page boys might be up to, whether the bridesmaids were shivering, or if her sumptuous silk gown was displayed to its best. In fact, the impression Julia had throughout the entire shoot was that Annabelle Kent would rather be somewhere, indeed anywhere, else.

'I'll have a man come round to mend the door,' Mrs. Kent was saying.

'No, really, there's no need —'

'Nonsense. It's our fault that you were broken into, Mrs. McAllister. I'll make sure you can lock up by close of business.'

Given that Julia's only interaction with the bride had been wedding photos, it was easy to forget that she was Theodore Parsons' only child, heiress to a booming toy manufactory. Even at the tender age of nineteen, capability radiated from every pore as Mrs. Kent reached for Julia's telephone without asking and issued instructions down the line.

'The set-back's only temporary,' Julia assured her, once she'd hung up. 'You'll still have your prints framed in ample time for Christmas.'

'They're not lost forever, then?'

'Heavens, no.' Julia ushered Mrs. Kent into the dark room and, credit where it's due, her pretty blonde visitor didn't so much as wince at the stench from the chemicals. 'These are the negatives. See?' Julia held the plates up to the light. 'I'll work through the night to —'

Mrs. Kent might not have winced, but crikey, she knew how to faint.

'Am I pregnant?' Mrs. Kent asked when she came round. 'All I want is babies, is that why I fainted? How long do you need to be carrying before the symptoms kick in?'

Julia's first thought was — *how the hell would I know?* Her second thought was — *this woman's only been married four days.* Her third was — *what she'd got up to beforehand is none of my business.* But thoughts are one thing. The priority was to shove a stiff brandy down the girl's throat. There was no time to brew tea, she was as white as a —

'Ghost.' The new bride sat up and pulled an apologetic face. 'Sorry about the baby thing. I've never fainted before and was completely disorientated, but — well — seeing the ghost threw me.'

Humour her, humour her, don't let her pass out a second time.

Sod that. Give her the brandy.

'I always knew I'd see him again.' It went down in one toss. 'Caleb, I mean.' Mrs. Kent smiled, and not purely because Julia refilled her glass. 'I'd loved him since I was six, is that silly?' She didn't wait for an answer. 'Papa didn't approve, of course. No matter how kind, or clever, or how well-respected, a blacksmith would never be good enough for his little girl.'

'Correct me if I'm wrong, Mrs. Kent —'

'Annabelle. Please. If I'm sitting on your darkroom floor, drinking your cognac and pouring my heart out, then the least we can do is dispense with formalities.'

'And possibly floors?' Julia held out a hand to help her up.

'I'm actually very comfortable.'

Julia slid down the wall, skirts pooling at her feet, wondering if insanity ran in the family. Hers, as much as Annabelle's.

'Sorry, what were you were saying before I interrupted?' Annabelle Kent asked.

'Only that you don't strike me as the type to march to other peoples' drums.'

'You mean marrying a man I don't love just so the factory will have a steady hand at the helm?' Down went the second shot. Out came a hand for a third. 'Well, that's the thing, Julia. I can call you Julia, can't I?' Once again, she didn't wait for an answer. 'After Caleb died, nothing mattered, and since the only thing I ever wanted was babies, tons of them, Barton Kent was the obvious choice. Not because he'd been trying to court me for months, or that he's always been Papa's first choice, because he's got a good head for figures and business. I married him for the simple reason that he's not bad to look at—'

He certainly wasn't.

'— so if I'm going to make babies with anyone now that Caleb is gone, it might as well be with someone attractive, and it doesn't matter that I don't care for Bart, I can throw my love into children, then this way, he and Papa can run the company, and I won't have that guilt hanging round my neck like an albatross. I hope I'm not embarrassing you with such intimate details, Julia, but quite honestly there's nobody else I can talk to.

'The thing is, Mama was terribly ill after I was born and the poor darling never recovered, which meant no more children, and so as far back as I can remember, Papa raised me to take over. Which, with him being such a terrible hypochondriac, he believes could happen any minute, which is nonsense; he's as fit as a fiddle. Oh, my, I must have spilled my cognac, could I trouble you — no, forget that, I'll help myself.'

'Listen, Annabelle. About Caleb —'

'Well, that's the thing, isn't it? Now everything from tools to chains to agricultural implements are mass-produced, and even canal barges run on steam, and of course hardly anyone keeps horses now that mechanical carriages are taking over, blacksmiths are pretty much obsolete. But I told Papa straight. I said, I don't care that it's a dying trade, and I don't care that I'd be living in what you would call poverty, but the instant I reach my majority, Caleb and I are getting married. And I'm sorry about the factory, truly I am, but I've told you all along I want nothing to do with it. I want to be a wife and a mother, not a captain of industry, and I love Caleb —'

'Yes. About that.'

'Only he's dead, he's dead, and I have to go on, and that'sh why I married Barton, becaush if I can't have a baby with —'

'Annabelle, stop!'

Julia was about to point out how cameras can't lie, and they most certainly can't take pictures of ghosts, but bless her, the newlywed had passed out again.

Only this time it wasn't from shock.

Sobering up heiresses is harder that you think. On the one hand, you can hardly call a hansom cab, scoop them inside, and have them delivered to their doorstep in that state. Equally, you don't want them clogging up the premises when you have work to do. And as wealthy and influential as Julia's pretty client was, Mr. Palmer's grief came first.

'His hair is crisp, and black, and long, his face is like the tan; His brow is wet with honest sweat, he earns whate'er he can,

And looks the whole world in the face, for he owes not any man,' came a slurred voice from the floor.

Damn! Julia was so busy measuring carbonate of potash with bromide of potassium and water to add to the developing fluid she'd already mixed in order to bring Mrs. Palmer's image into focus that she'd forgotten to remove the bottle from next to where she'd left Annabelle snoring away on her darkroom floor.

'Longfellow?' Julia said, tugging the brandy out of Annabelle's fist.

Annabelle nodded blearily. 'He understood,' she slurred. 'He understood that it's not shameful to be a blacksmith. That it's a proud and honest trade, but ... but ... when his smithy burns to the ground ... and my Caleb's inside... Why did he leave me, Julia? How could he die and leave me alive? How could he do this to me?'

Damn, damn, damn.

Cradling the sobbing bride, rocking her in her arms, Julia thought, *so much for tidings of comfort and joy.* Now she had not one, but two broken hearts on her hands.

Outside, in the bleak mid-winter, frosty wind made moan.

Henry Longfellow also said that into each life, some rain must fall. In Annabelle Kent's, it was pouring. Over several cups of strong coffee, along with half a madeira cake to mop up the booze, the story came tumbling out. Her love for the blacksmith. His love for her. A love that overrode duty and all practicality, but that's what happens when two souls fuse into one. Anything — everything — becomes insurmountable.

Everything, that is, except death.

Julia remembered reading about it in the papers three months ago. How the fire brigade was called out in the wee small hours, and despite every engine pumping out two hundred gallons a minute, the inferno was too fierce to save Caleb Norton. The poor man was trapped when a beam collapsed, and, considering his strength and youth, it was believed this had knocked him out cold, explaining the lack of cries for help. A blessing in disguise, in its way.

'Papa identified the body.'

It was partly to save her the pain, Annabelle said, but also because he knew Caleb from when he was born — the smithy being next door to his first workshop, long before he turned to churning out tiny toys alongside whistles and paper hats to go inside Christmas crackers and needed to expand — and Caleb had no family.

'Papa used his father's services a great deal in the old days, which is how I spent so much time there. Even at that age, Papa insisted on showing me the business, and I pretended to be interested so I could hang around Caleb. When his father died a year or so after the factory opened, it was the perfect excuse to spend even more time there.' She blew her nose. 'Like I said, Papa was pretty cut up about the fire. Especially when he had to identify the remains. But not,' she snapped, 'cut up enough to stop Barton Kent publishing the banns for our marriage without so much as consulting me.'

That's where grief makes such a mess of things, Julia thought. Right at the point where you think life can't get any worse, it spurs you into rash — and usually poor — decisions. Some people turn to drink, a spiral not everyone climbs back from. Others find peace in laudanum. Another slippery slope. Work might appear to be the perfect antidote, but all work and no play doesn't lead to dullness. It leads to malnutrition, obsession, foul temper and, far too often, apoplexy or compression on the heart. Unfortunately, there is no quick repair for heartbreak, and Annabelle wasn't the first person to jump into marriage as a misguided channel to recovery, and she certainly wouldn't be the last. The need to feel loved in times of loss is overwhelming. Just a shame it's not discriminating.

But strong as it was, that bitter northerly wind hadn't jemmied Julia's door, and it certainly hadn't stolen the Kents' wedding photos. Holding the negative up to the light, Annabelle thought she'd seen Caleb's ghost, but ghosts don't hide behind yew trees in the churchyard. So if Caleb was alive, why didn't he rush straight to the woman he loved? Why break in and steal the prints of her wedding?

And most importantly, who really died in the fire?

Once upon a time, Oakbourne was a sedate little town on the far west side of London. It had a pretty Saxon church, winding cobbled streets, and was flanked by the bourne — the stream — from which it got its name. That was until the long, cumbersome lines of pack horses and carts were supplanted by canals, slashing both time and transportation costs, and cutting coal prices by three quarters. By the time Alfred Lord Tennyson was appointed Poet Laureate in 1850, nearly five thousand miles of canals were criss-crossing Britain, and while Oakbourne proved a perfect link to the busiest of them all, the Grand Union and therefore the London docks, life didn't really change until the railways moved in.

Now, almost half a century on, it had become a town of two halves, with suburbs, shops and a lovely wide Common on one side, and dark factories, mills and slums on the other, belching out smoke, poverty, homelessness and crime. The two worlds separated by a watery highway, on which barges chased cargo and families slept in cabins the size of dog kennels. Today, if you wanted to see farmlands and fields, you had to take the train, but perhaps the biggest impact on Oakbourne was its exploding population.

And nothing said how much those numbers had expanded as much as the streets just three days before Christmas.

'*O come, all ye faithful...*'

Carol singers were on every corner, some with pipes, some with drums, some with handbells, some with the whole damn shooting match. There were stalls touting every living creature from monkeys with chains round their necks to parrots in cages to dormice and hedgehogs. Men struggled through the crowds with dolls' houses, clockwork toys and rocking horses. Women juggled wreaths of holly and ivy to hang over the windows, and sprigs of mistletoe to hang inside the door. Turkeys that left Norfolk in October, to be walked all the way then fattened up once they arrived, now hung outside the butcher's shops, ready for the next phase in their lives. Stuffing.

'Where, exactly, are we going?' Annabelle asked, as the hansom clopped over the bridge. 'All you said on the telephone was to come to the studio to collect the prints, but bring a cab, as you had something to show me.'

'Which I have,' Julia said. 'We're nearly there.'

Julia had not been idle since their last meeting. Admittedly, a disproportionate amount of time was spent feeding a small feline with a predilection for ham, clotted cream, offal and herrings, all of which Julia had bought specially. And all of which was well worth the expenditure, given that the tabby's ribs no longer poked through.

The darkroom had taken up much of her time, too. Mr. Palmer was pleased, not to mention comforted, with Julia's portrait. He jumped at her suggestion to smuggle in the body of his stillborn son to hide under his wife's skirts, that they might be buried together. And while Julia couldn't help but pity the men tasked with digging a grave in this iron-hard earth, her prime focus was on Annabelle Kent.

Just like the first time when she developed the prints, Julia was struck by the detailed embroidery on the bride's gown, the matching turban and long, floaty veil. But whereas before, when she'd imagined the excitement in the Parsons household before heading off to church, as her hair was arranged and majestic bouquet tweaked while maids fluffed miles of cream silk, she had a new perspective on Annabelle's seemingly indifferent air. It was not because she was an heiress, raised to keep her exhilaration in check. But because she was an heiress, raised to keep *every emotion* in check.

Developing, of course, is a time-consuming business, never mind with Christmas knocking on the door. Which meant fetching sprigs of greenery to dot round her shop, decorating them with ribbons and bows, hanging glittery baubles in the window, along with an eight-point silver star with a pretty embossed cherub centre stage. There were cards to write out. Invitations to post. Holly and ivy to lay on Sam Whitmore's grave, a silly superstition about protecting his soul from evil, but honestly, who would take chances?

As busy as she was, though, there was still one more job Julia had to do.

'We're here,' she said, nudging Annabelle with her elbow.

'Where?'

'The place where ghosts live.'

'Caleb?'

'Pixie!'

Seeing the couple rush into one another's arms brought a ridiculously large lump to Julia's throat, even though their reunion was exactly how she'd imagined it.

'I thought you were dead.'

'Oh, my darling, my love! Why would you think that?'

That was the very question Julia had been asking herself. Why indeed? Watching them hug and cry, and hold each other like they'd never let go, she wished there could be a happier ending to this tragic *Romeo and Juliet* story.

It hadn't taken long to track Caleb down. Like Annabelle said, blacksmiths were a dying breed, now that most metal implements were mass-produced in the factories. But dying isn't the same as dead, and it was thinking about the hansom cab that she couldn't call to take intoxicated new brides home that gave her the idea. With the rise in population came a rise in the number of cabs. Cabs are pulled by horses. And horses, of course, need shoes.

'Why didn't you come to me?' Annabelle wailed. 'Why didn't you come to me after the fire?'

'What was the point? I was fitting wrought-iron railings over at Bentley-on-Thames when it happened, and that was a four-day job. When I got back, the place was burned to a cinder, then Barton turns up while I'm sorting through the wreckage, tells me to stay clear of you from now on. How you decided to put duty above everything else, that you're marrying him, then shows me the announcement in the papers to prove it. What am I supposed to think, eh? Four days after some tramp dosses in my place, burns it to the ground accidentally and dies in the process, poor bugger, you're posting the banns —'

'Wait!' Annabelle sprang back as though she'd been scalded. 'Barton came to see you? B-b-but if Bart knew all along that you were alive…'

The only person who could have told him that was her father.

'Pixie, Pixie, Pixie.' For a big man, the blacksmith could certainly churn out the tears. 'I've loved you since you were six, you know that. But your father was right. You deserve better than me. You have a destiny, Annabelle —'

'Overseeing love notes and whistles stuffed inside crackers, making sure they go bang when they're pulled?'

'Very well, you have a responsibility. And whether Kent tricked you or not, you're a married woman. You need to go back to your husband.'

Later, Julia couldn't be sure whether Annabelle had said not on your nelly or bugger that. Possibly both. Either way, she made it abundantly clear to the driver that there would be only one passenger on the return journey. And quite frankly, the kiss between her and Caleb was hot enough to burn his new place down.

Julia pulled down the blinds on her shop and poured herself a glass of mulled wine.

What would happen to Joseph Parsons was anyone's guess.

Did he conspire with Barton Kent to burn down the smithy, knowing Caleb wouldn't have the funds to rebuild, forcing him to take a job out of the area and thereby leaving the way clear for Barton to marry his daughter?

Quite likely, because when Julia went to take a look at the ruined smithy, a bunch of scruffy urchins were doing what bunches of scruffy urchins always do — playing in the street. And it's amazing what a few little oiks can let slip over a quarter pound of toffees and three sticks of barley sugar apiece just before Christmas.

Like the "two toffs" they saw hanging around the night of the fire. And the unmistakeable smell of liquid paraffin.

Papa was pretty cut up about the fire. Especially when he had to identify the remains.

Damn right he was! He'd timed the attack for when the son of his old friend would be out of town, so imagine finding some drunk had stumbled in, passed out, then been trapped by a falling beam, which is what Julia imagined had happened.

But whether it was just him on his own or with Barton Kent at his side, Joseph Parsons remained an arsonist and a killer.

Should she call the police, or let Annabelle do it? Julia knew Annabelle would. Make no mistake, the girl who Parsons had raised to take over — the girl who picked up the phone without asking and had the broken lock fixed — would not flinch. Partly because both men had betrayed her, and didn't care about the pain they'd inflicted. Partly because they callously set out to ruin a good man for their own selfish ends. But mainly because a man died at their hands.

'So then, Tabs.' Julia stroked the little cat coiled up on her lap, with not a rib to be felt. 'What do you reckon?'

Sipping spiced wine while carol singers jingled their bells under her window, she flipped through the prints of the Kents' wedding. Killer father. Conspiring husband. Jilted lover watching events from the bushes, then stealing the photos in case he'd been spotted. No one's going to pick up the tab for these now.

'Back to taking naughty pictures to pay for your cream?'

The only sound was a loud, rattling purr.

Julia took that for a yes.

Intrigued by England's first crime scene photographer?
Start reading the Julia McAllister Victorian Mysteries
now!

Connect with Marilyn Todd!
Facebook/MarilynToddCrimeWriter
Twitter: @MarilynTodd12
www.marilyntodd.com

CHRISTMAS SPIRITS BY GAYNOR TORRANCE

Cardiff, Wales, 2019

Detective Inspector Jemima Huxley was sinking under the weight of pre-Christmas guilt. Despite vowing to be better organised this year, the very nature of her job made it virtually impossible for her to feel as though she was doing justice to any aspect of her home life. There was an ever-growing list of things Jemima needed to get on top of before the big day. And that was in addition to her role as a stepparent, which she didn't take lightly.

From the moment he entered her life, young James had been a beacon of light. An antidote to the darkness and depravity she regularly had to deal with. And no matter how bad her day had been, the young boy's infectious *joie de vivre* made her laugh and feel like a child again. His presence really was a godsend, given the terrible situations she often encountered at work.

Jemima loved James as though he were her own, and was determined to do her best for him. But during the festive season, her resolve came at a hefty price. There were school concerts, carol services, and county orchestra events to attend. And somehow she had accidentally volunteered to help sort and deliver hundreds of Christmas cards for the annual scout post.

It was all too much. If Jemima had been a stay-at-home parent, it might have been easier to take things in her stride. But Jemima's job was more pressurised and unpredictable than most, with no set clocking off time. And it seemed as though in the run-up to the festivities her entire existence had become an unrelenting exercise in time management. So much so, that being at work came as a welcome relief.

The weather that morning was cold and dry. There had been a sharp frost the night before, leaving the air crisp and perhaps fresher than you'd expect it to be in a city. Jemima and Sergeant Dan Broadbent had spent the last few hours on a wild goose chase. They'd received an anonymous tip-off that Mick Robinson, the main suspect in a recent murder, had been spotted in the vicinity of the Norwegian Church.

The pair had headed to Cardiff Bay to scour the area, cursing its close proximity to the Welsh Government's Senedd building, as it was such a popular location. The timing couldn't have been worse, as a large number of school children and their teachers had gathered there to sing Christmas carols. Assembly Members were scheduled to join them before the politicians returned home for the Christmas recess. And, unsurprisingly, BBC Wales had decided to cover the event, as it was a festive news item taking place on their doorstep.

After a few hours of what turned out to be a futile search, Jemima and Broadbent positioned themselves near the Senedd steps to keep an eye out for Robinson, on the off-chance that he should turn up. They both knew that it was highly unlikely, as any suspect on the run would hardly choose to hang out at an event where there was going to be live news coverage.

The wind had picked up and a biting breeze slapped mercilessly at any exposed skin of those braving the elements. It also skimmed the surface of the freshwater lake, causing grey ripples to rise and swell as though some substantial life form was lurking in the murky depths below.

'Remind me why we're doing this? It's a waste of time and my toes are starting to go numb,' muttered Broadbent, as he shoved his hands deeper into the pockets of his padded jacket, whilst hopping from foot to foot in a bid to keep warm.

'If Mick Robinson turned up and attacked someone after we headed back, we'd both be for the high jump, so stop moaning,' hissed Jemima, aware that her breath was visible as she spoke. She wasn't immune to the cold and wished that they were back at the station too. But it was what it was. 'Just look at those kids. They're so excited. That could be your Harry in a few years.'

'Not likely. I'm not going to allow him to freeze to death just to make some mediocre politicians look good for the cameras.'

'Oh, bah humbug! With an attitude like that, Christmas won't be up to much at your house,' said Jemima, shaking her head in despair.

'Song sheets?' asked a middle-aged woman as she headed towards them, waving pieces of paper.

'Not likely,' said Broadbent sullenly, refusing to take his hands out of his pockets.

'He'll share mine,' said Jemima, as she flashed the woman her sweetest smile and reached out to take one of the sheets.

'Don't expect me to sing,' muttered Broadbent.

'Well, if you don't, you're going to stand out like a sore thumb when the camera pans across this way.'

Almost an hour later, they were both colder than they had ever thought possible. The crowd had dispersed and Jemima and Broadbent headed back to their unmarked police car.

'I need a fag,' said Broadbent as he rummaged in his pocket and pulled out a packet of cigarettes along with a disposable lighter.

'Oh no you don't! Caroline told me to confiscate them if I ever saw you smoking again. And I know from past experience not to cross your wife. So come on, hand them over.' Jemima held out her hand as though she was about to take contraband from a naughty child.

'You're my boss, not my mother,' moaned Broadbent, as he reluctantly placed the items in Jemima's hand. 'Don't let on to Caro, though. She'll give me hell.'

'It's because she loves you. Though I don't know why. I think she needs her head testing. Anyway, it's your turn to drive.' Jemima placed the offending items in one of her coat pockets and tossed her partner the car key.

As they set off towards the police station, they came across a recently erected diversion sign informing drivers that the road ahead was closed. The alternative route would add a couple of miles to the journey, but the heater was blowing out warm air, so it wasn't such an inconvenience.

'Hey, it's that toy shop that everyone's raving about!' shouted Jemima, as they approached a retail park. 'Pull in so we can take a look. It'll be quieter at this time of day. It's way better than going there at the weekend.'

'Never thought I'd see the day when you'd put Christmas shopping above work.'

'Oh, stop complaining. We'll be fifteen minutes, thirty tops. No one will ever know.'

'I'm not complaining. There're a few things I'd like to pick up for Harry. So it's fine with me. I'll keep shtum if you do,' said Broadbent, with a mischievous twinkle in his eye.

To refer to the place as a shop didn't do it justice, as it was an out-of-town retail unit of vast proportions. The interior was every parent's nightmare and a child's idea of heaven, as there was so much choice, with price tags to make your eyes water.

As they parked up, it was unclear whether the place was open. The window shutters were still down, but the door was ajar. From inside the car, they could hear Christmas music playing loudly throughout the store, and as they walked towards the entrance they spotted a few people, presumably members of staff, dressed as elves.

'Looks as though it's only just opening,' said Broadbent, nodding toward some other customers heading for the entrance.

'Great. At least it should be quiet. Meet you back at the car in twenty,' said Jemima as they crossed the threshold together, then immediately went their separate ways.

Jemima wandered down an aisle, humming 'Rockin' Around the Christmas Tree', as the lyrics belted out over the store's sound system. It seemed that wherever you went at this time of year, you were bombarded with feel-good music, designed to get you into the festive spirit and loosen the grip on the purse strings.

There were so many children that Jemima had to buy presents for. As well as James, there were her sister's three kids and Broadbent's little lad, Harry, who also happened to be Jemima's godson. James had already written an exceptionally long wishlist. And Jemima's sister, Lucy, had given her a few options for each of her offspring. As for Harry, well, she would be guided by Broadbent on that one.

Jemima took out her phone, tapped the screen and studied the list of presents. She was out of touch with children's toys and had no idea what many of the things were. As they had no business taking time out to go shopping, she thought it would be more efficient to track down a member of staff and ask them to point her in the right direction. At least the assistants would be easy to spot, as they were dressed as elves.

She looked around and saw one up ahead, marching towards the far end of the aisle. 'Excuse me!' she called, only to be ignored. The elf didn't turn around and just kept on walking.

Jemima was used to getting people's attention and had no intention of being overlooked. She picked up her pace. 'Excuse me! I need some help!' she called. When she was ignored yet again, she began to jog towards the back of the shop. But before she caught up with the unhelpful assistant, he disappeared through a set of double doors into the stockroom at the rear of the store.

Jemima was annoyed. He needed some customer service training. She decided to find out the assistant's name then report them to the store manager. But before she reached the doors, they opened again. Three men dressed as elves walked out. Each carried a large, unmarked box, which from the way they were walking, gave the appearance of being heavy.

Jemima stood and stared as they headed towards her.

'Why are there people in the shop?' hissed the first elf. 'I told you not to open up until we were out of 'ere.'

'I gave the key to one of your lot,' said the elf at the rear.

'That's right, he did. Beasley had it,' said the middle elf.

'Typical. I knew I shouldn't 'ave let 'im in on this. If anything goes wrong. I swear to God...'

'Take a chill pill. One more trip to the van should do it. We'll be outta 'ere in ten,' said the second elf, clearly trying to placate the man in charge.

'Where's Beasley now? Ee s'posed to be 'elpin' us,' grunted the leader.

'Dunno, 'aven't seen him. Probably gone lookin' for somethin' for that kid of 'is,' replied the second elf.

Up close, Jemima could see that the first two men were big, muscular and looked far from friendly. The leader had an angry red scar on his left cheek, which made him appear more pantomime villain than Santa's little helper. These were not the sort of men you would expect to find working in a toy shop.

As Jemima mused on these thoughts, the elf bringing up the rear approached her. He was smaller than his companions and, unlike the other two, he looked straight at her. She noticed beads of sweat on his brow, an ugly bruise on his cheek and a distinct look of fear in his eyes. But before she had a chance for further thought, he walked on.

Jemima had been a police officer for long enough to know when something was wrong. And as nothing appeared to be awry inside the shop, then whatever was going down must surely be happening in the stockroom.

Christmas shopping would have to wait.

Jemima made a beeline for the end of the aisle as she tried to find Broadbent. As she walked, she speed-dialled Detective Chief Inspector Ray Kennedy's number.

'Broadbent and I are at Marchmont Toy Emporium,' she told him when he answered. 'Something's going down, but I'm not sure what it is. There're at least three suspects, possibly more. We need backup. Any idea how long it'll be before they arrive?'

'Best guess of fifteen minutes,' replied Kennedy. 'Are the suspects armed?'

'I don't know, and I don't think they're planning on hanging around.'

'Well, keep a low profile. See what you can find out, but no heroics. I don't want anyone getting hurt,' ordered Kennedy.

Jemima scanned the aisles, but there was still no sign of Broadbent. It was so typical of her partner. She sometimes thought he disappeared on purpose. She was about to dial his number when she heard a ruckus coming from a nearby aisle. She lengthened her stride to what was now a reasonably brisk walk, conscious of the fact that she didn't want to attract any unwanted attention.

The voices became higher, louder and more aggressive, as the confrontation ratcheted up. When Jemima reached the aisle where the argument had kicked off, she could see that two men were arguing over a toy. Broadbent was already in the middle of it, doing his best to try to diffuse the situation.

'Gerroff!' snarled the shorter of the two men, as he tightened his grip on a box. It didn't take a genius to realise that he was not someone to be messed with. He was lean, wiry, and his pointy features enhanced a feral expression. His eyes narrowed, glinting demonically as he stared his opposition down, and as his lips curled back, they revealed badly discoloured teeth. 'I — said — gerroff!' he demanded as he tugged even harder.

'I saw it first! So it's mine!' yelled the other man, showing no inclination to loosen his grip on the box.

'No it's not,' snapped the smaller man, who, without warning, headbutted his opponent.

The taller man staggered backwards but remained upright. When he noticed the blood spurting from his nose, he let go of the box. 'D-did you see that?' he squealed. 'Did you see what that maniac just did to me? I'll have you for that! I'll bloody have you! That was assault, and I've got witnesses!' he shouted.

'Yeah, yeah!' said the aggressor, without a backwards glance. He was already swaggering away with the box tucked neatly under his arm.

Jemima realised that any second now, Broadbent would arrest the thug. But, with whatever was going down in the store, she couldn't afford to let him do that. She needed to get there before her partner identified himself as a police officer.

'Dan!' she called, hoping to attract his attention, but it was too late.

Broadbent set off like a whippet out of the trap. 'Stop! Police!' he yelled.

'Ya want some too, d'ya!' yelled the man as he spun around to confront Broadbent.

'You're under arrest for common assault. Anything you say will be —'

'Fink I'm afraid a you? Fink again. I've laid out men twice your size, so I don't fancy your chances. This is my kid's present! No one else's. It's pafetic tryin' ta make me fink you're a copper. So back off and you won't leave 'ere with a busted face like ya mate there,' the man snarled.

'Don't make things worse for yourself. You do not want to attack a police officer,' said Broadbent, as he calmly extracted a set of handcuffs from his waistband and continued to caution the man.

'Oh yeah, I do,' snarled the guy. He dropped the box on the floor and launched himself at Broadbent, who ended up flat on his back with his assailant on top of him. With lightning speed, the man landed a powerful punch, square on Broadbent's face.

Jemima was left with no choice. She had to get involved, otherwise Broadbent would end up getting battered. So much for keeping a low profile until the reinforcements arrived. In the seconds it took for Jemima to reach them, the man's elbow was raised in readiness to hit Broadbent for the second time.

'Oh no you don't!' yelled Jemima, grabbing his raised arm firmly and yanking it backwards. She reached for Broadbent's set of handcuffs and expertly clipped the thug's hands behind his back.

'Gerroff me, you mad bitch,' he whined.

There was the sound of running feet and the first two elves that Jemima had previously spotted came dashing up the aisle towards them.

'They're coppers!' warned the man in handcuffs.

'What're ya doin', Beasley?' bellowed the scarred elf. 'And why aren't you dressed like the rest a us? You shoulda been 'elpin' ta shift the boxes. Not messin' round wif kid's toys! And you lot shouldn't have poked your noses into our business,' he growled, turning his attention to Jemima, Broadbent, and the handful of customers who had come to see what was happening. 'A few more minutes and we'da bin outta 'ere. No one woulda got 'urt. But that's all changed now. This muppet's seen to that —' he kicked out at Beasley and connected with the man's shin. 'Look, I don't wanna 'urt anyone. So uncuff 'im, then get in the back,' he ordered.

'I can't do that. I don't have the key,' said Jemima.

'You've gotta be jokin',' snarled the elf. He removed a gun from his trouser pocket and pointed it at Jemima. ''Spect me ta believe tha'?'

Suddenly the situation had become a whole lot more dangerous.

'They're not my cuffs,' she replied, doing her best to stop her voice from trembling.

'They're mine,' spluttered Broadbent.

'So unlock them, soft lad.'

Broadbent staggered to his feet. The punch had shaken him. He felt inside his pockets. 'It's not there,' he mumbled.

'Wha' d'ya mean, it's not there?' said the man with the gun.

'It must have fallen out of my pocket when he pushed me over,' said Broadbent. 'It's got to be around here somewhere.'

'Lock tha door! Do it now, or I swear ta god I'm goin' ta shoot someone. And don't ya fink of doin' a runner, 'cos ya know what'll 'appen if ya do,' the man with the gun snarled. 'Everyone in the back, now!' he yelled, waving his gun menacingly.

As he issued the order, a female customer suddenly made a break for it and started to run towards the doors. The gunman tilted his weapon and fired it at the ceiling. Realising that there was no chance of escape, the woman skidded to a halt and began to howl like a banshee.

'Shut it, you stupid bint!' he snarled. 'Try some'in' like tha' again an' I'll shoot ya dead. Get yourself back up 'ere with the others. C'mon, move it!'

The woman scuttled towards them, keeping her head down so as not to look at the man or the gun. Jemima could see that she was petrified.

'Don't kill me. I've got a child,' she wailed.

'Yeah? Well, we've all got kids, darlin'. Don' make ya special. Now get in tha back. Move it! You too, mister-toy-shop-manager,' he snarled, pointing his weapon at the scared elf, who, having done as he was told, had locked the door then returned.

As they made their way towards the stockroom, Jemima could see that the skin around Broadbent's eyes was already beginning to swell. Soon the injury would affect his vision and leave him next-to-useless. If they were to stand any chance against these armed thugs, it would be down to her to go it alone.

'Speed it up! I ain't got all day,' ordered the gunman, as he jabbed the weapon into the woman's back, causing her to wail even louder.

'There's no need for that. Leave her alone. Can't you see she's scared?' said Broadbent.

'Shut it, copper. Or it won' just be a busted 'oota you've got to worry 'bout. I 'ain't shot anyone yet. But I might just make a' exception in your case since you messed me roun' like this.' He turned to his deputy and tossed him a set of keys. 'Get tha last box to tha van. An' take Beasley with ya. I'll join ya when I've sorted this lot out.'

There was no time to waste. As the other two thugs had headed off to the getaway vehicle, only one man posed an immediate threat — though Jemima knew he was armed and dangerous. Having innocent civilians caught up in this added to the complexity of the problem.

Jemima knew that she'd only get one chance to disarm the gunman. If she messed up, things could quickly get a whole lot more dangerous. It was a situation where people could be injured or even die. But she couldn't afford to wait until backup arrived. To have any chance of this ending well, Jemima needed to go in hard and fast, and take him by surprise.

The moment she set foot in the stockroom, Jemima had quickly assessed the area. She noticed that two women and a man were gagged and tied to chairs. There was also an unmistakable smell of alcohol. It was not something you would expect to find in a toy shop. On the floor up ahead was some shattered glass and a broken box. The cardboard was dark and soggy, and the surrounding floor was wet.

'I shouldn't be here! Pleeeease, let me go. I won't say anything to anyone,' begged the female customer.

In the time it had taken them to walk into the stockroom the woman's fear had become almost full-blown hysteria. Jemima knew that if it remained unchecked, there was a genuine possibility that the woman would totally freak out. And if that happened, it could push the thug to shoot her, just to shut her up.

In a situation such as this, it was in everyone's interest to stay calm and not provoke a reaction from a gunman. But for what Jemima had in mind, she needed to cause a distraction.

Jemima discreetly slipped a hand inside her coat pocket and felt around until her fingers located Broadbent's lighter and the packet of cigarettes.

'You're startin' ta do ma 'ed in. Shut ya mouth, or I'll shut it for ya!' yelled the leader. His face was only inches from the woman's. As he shouted, spittle landed on her cheek.

The woman cringed, closed her eyes and began to sob loudly.

Jemima realised that it was now or never. She whipped out the lighter and the packet of cigarettes. Placing her hands behind her back, she flicked the lighter until she felt the packaging get warm. Broadbent saw what she was up to and nodded, almost imperceptibly, to let her know that he understood what she was about to do.

Jemima knew, without looking, that the packaging was alight. Her fingers were painfully hot as the small flame grew and licked her skin. There was not a moment to lose, as she couldn't hold onto it for much longer. She spun around and hurled the burning package, aiming for the spilt liquor. There was a split second as she watched it fly through the air when she thought that maybe her aim was a little off. Or the flame would extinguish itself before it reached the intended target. She knew that if she missed the mark, it could have catastrophic repercussions for all of them. But she needn't have worried. The packet was almost full, giving it enough weight to remain airborne for the required distance.

There was an ominous *whoooooosh* as the missile landed and the alcohol ignited.

'Wha' tha —' began the man with the gun. His jaw dropped in disbelief and his grip on the weapon momentarily relaxed, the muzzle of the firearm drooping towards the floor.

Over the last few years, Jemima had worked hard on improving her personal fitness. Part of the gruelling regime she put herself through was to have weekly training sessions with a fellow police officer, who just happened to be an expert kickboxer. It was often agonising and always exhausting, but Jemima enjoyed the physical challenge it provided. And it gave her the self-confidence to take on and overcome an assailant in a situation such as this.

With lightning speed, Jemima moved towards her opponent, who was distracted by the flames and didn't see her coming. She went in hard and fast, putting the full force of her body into the attack as she turned and jabbed the side of his head. The contact was so powerful that it set him off balance. Miraculously, he dropped the gun and it skittered across the floor.

Without allowing her opponent time to draw breath, Jemima followed up with a right cross then a roundhouse kick, which floored him. He dropped like a stone and was still disoriented as her knees landed on the small of his back, causing him to cry out in pain. Jemima allowed herself a smile of satisfaction as she used her own set of handcuffs to restrain him.

'You're nicked,' she snarled as the fire alarm blared and the sprinkler system delivered a deluge of water.

Broadbent wasted no time retrieving the gun, while the shop manager rushed to free his colleagues then used a fire extinguisher to help put out the blaze.

As the group emerged from the stockroom, wet and shaken, they were met by the reinforcements that Detective Chief Inspector Kennedy had sent. Beasley and his accomplice had already been arrested and were both locked securely inside a police van. In the time it took everyone to reach the main entrance the fire brigade had arrived.

Investigations revealed that the gang were responsible for a string of robberies at off-licences throughout the area. They had stopped at the retail park shortly before six o'clock that morning when their vehicle's engine overheated and they were unable to restart it.

In his statement, the manager of the toy shop confirmed that as he and his staff arrived for work that day, they encountered the men acting suspiciously. The manager was about to call the police when the thugs spotted them and marched them at gunpoint into the shop, which was where they spent the rest of the morning.

The gang had tied up the shop workers and told the manager that his colleagues would be shot if he didn't cooperate with them. They carried the boxes of alcohol into the stockroom whilst they waited for a replacement vehicle. Unfortunately for everyone concerned, things didn't go to plan — the other vehicle took far longer than anticipated to arrive.

Back at the station, Jemima and Broadbent walked into the squad room to whistles and applause.

'Let's hear it for the superstars!' shouted Detective Constable Gareth Peters.

'What's going on?' asked Jemima, completely bewildered.

'You're both the talk of the station. We've seen a BBC clip of the two of you singing carols down at the Bay. Have you ever thought of auditioning for *Britain's Got Talent*? Perhaps you could try a festive duet? Something like, "Rudolph the Red-Nosed Reindeer"?' said Peters. Doing his best to keep a straight face, he pointed at Broadbent's swollen nose.

Everyone fell about laughing.

'Oh, ha, bloody ha,' said Broadbent.

'Dan, you really need to lighten up and get some Christmas spirit,' said Jemima, still laughing. 'At this time of year, you should really say "ho, ho, ho".'

Want to solve more cases with DI Huxley?
Get the first book in the DI Jemima Huxley Investigations series now!

Connect with Gaynor Torrance!
Facebook/GaynorTorranceAuthor
Twitter: @GaytorAuthor
www.gaynortorrance.com

THE ESSEX NATIVITY BY DAVID FIELD

Essex, England, 1895

Jack Enright smiled with satisfaction as he signed off on his last report for 1895 and sat back in his office chair to contemplate the ten days of leave that he now had ahead of him. Jack had completed his first three months as the Detective Sergeant at Essex Constabulary's woefully understaffed Detective Branch, and he was now looking forward to buying last-minute Christmas presents in time for the traditional family gathering at his mother Constance's house.

He and his wife Esther had hoped to break with tradition by holding the family gathering in their new home, but quite apart from his mother's outrage at the mere suggestion, there was a practical reason for opting for the old family home. While Jack and Esther's latest arrival, Miriam, was still less than a year old, and would be content with swirling items that tinkled above her cot, their older two children had much grander presents in mind. For the oldest of their offspring, five-year-old Lily, it had to be a complete dolls' house or nothing, while three-year-old Bertie had his heart set on a rocking horse. It would be impossible to hide presents of that size from inquisitive young eyes in Jack and Esther's own home, so they had no choice but to house the presents in Jack's old bedroom at Constance's house.

Jack was also planning a large present for Esther: a wall cabinet with a built-in sewing machine. Esther had tentatively asked for one or the other, and Jack had spent most of his dinner breaks scouring the limited range of stores in Chelmsford, until one day he'd found the two combined in a heavy oak piece in Tanner's Antiques. The purchase price was outrageous, but a few furtive enquiries among family members had resulted in the decision that they would all 'muck in' to buy it. Jack's Uncle Percy was due to arrive shortly to help with the arrangements for a carrier to take it down to Barking.

Percy Enright bustled in with a wide grin. The Chelmsford police canteen was putting on a Christmas Dinner a week ahead of the official day, and Jack had wisely chosen this day to coax his uncle — with his legendary appetite — from his lair in Scotland Yard. Percy had helped to raise Jack after his father's death, and it had been Percy's career in the police force which had inspired Jack's own. Percy had recently been moved to the political section of Scotland Yard, dealing with the scandals of the wealthy elite.

'So how's life in the Political Branch?' Jack asked Percy, as he watched turkey disappearing fast into his uncle's jaws.

Percy cleared his mouth, then grimaced. 'I may as well be back in "Burglaries".'

'What — thefts of spoons from the House of Lords Dining Room?' Jack joked.

Percy continued to frown. 'Not quite, but not far off. Break-ins at the London houses of senior politicians while they're attending late-night sessions with their wives. That's the suspicious bit, since only Parliamentary Officers would know when seats have been booked in the gallery for the wives, and therefore which family homes will be empty.'

'It's not much different down here, if it's any consolation,' Jack told him. 'But ours are less lofty — mainly wealthy outlying farms and suchlike, and the targets are farm machinery and animals. Half the butchers in Essex are probably selling stolen Christmas turkeys. Talking of which, let's have a quick cup of tea to wash down this dinner, then we need to take your cheque book for a walk.'

They'd almost made it through the front door when Jack was called back by the Desk Sergeant.

'Sorry an' all that, sir, but we've just 'ad word of a break-in over in Baddow Magna — a Colonel Channing who sez one've 'is farm'ands just spotted movement in an outbuildin' on 'is property.'

Jack thought quickly. 'Get the coach round to the front door and I'll deal with it immediately. Inspector Enright from Scotland Yard can assist. Burglary's his speciality at the moment.'

'Do we have to?' Percy complained as the police coach ground through the gathering sleet down the country lane into the small village where Colonel and Mrs Channing had their extensive farm and riding stables.

'No choice, I'm afraid,' Jack replied. 'I'm still on duty until five o'clock today — one of my constables is on sick leave, and the other's investigating a serious assault in Harlow. But we can still be back in town early enough to buy Esther's present, so keep your cheque book handy.'

As they alighted from the coach, one of three waiting farmhands ran over, doffed his cap and introduced himself. 'Amos Barker, sirs — the Colonel's senior livestock manager. There's somebody movin' around in that barn over there.'

'You two come with me,' Percy ordered the remaining farmhands as he instinctively took command of the situation. 'You, Mr Barker, go round the back with the Sergeant here.'

Doubling over to reduce his visibility, Percy pushed open the unlocked barn door, then cursed under his breath as it squeaked loudly and a scared face peered round the side of what had once been a horse stall.

Percy held his police badge high in the air and commanded the man to remain where he was. 'Right,' he added as he approached the man, 'who the Hell are you, and what are you about?'

'Joe Verney, sir — woodworker from out Maldon way. We just come in ter get warm, 'onest. It's comin' on ter snow, an' this time o' year it won't be long afore it's dark.'

'We?' Percy echoed. 'There's more than one of you, you mean?'

'Only Martha, back there, sir. She looks ter be about ter drop the baby, an' we'll need somewhere warm ter keep it.'

At that moment, Jack came hurrying through from the back of the barn, Amos Barker at his heels, white-faced. 'There's a young woman lying back there,' he announced, breathless with apprehension, 'and she reckons she's about to give birth!'

Percy looked across at Amos Barker. 'I take it there's a telephone at the house?'

'O' course,' Amos confirmed. 'That's 'ow we was able ter contact you lot.'

'Get back up there and call for the doctor,' Percy instructed him, then as Amos scuttled off Percy smiled at Jack. 'Did you deliver any of yours?'

Jack screwed up his face. 'What do you think?'

'It was worth a try. Anyway, go and give the poor woman what assistance you can.' Then Percy turned to Joe Verney and demanded more information regarding how he and Martha came to be where they were.

The story that emerged was the usual sad tale of a domestic servant 'caught out' with an unwanted pregnancy that had led to not only dismissal from her position as housemaid to a country lawyer and his family, but also rejection by her own scandalised parents. She and Joe had taken to the road two weeks previously, sleeping in outlying barns, begging food at farmhouse kitchen doors, and apprehensive of the winter that was rapidly closing in on Martha's impending childbirth. But Joe was insistent that they'd never once stooped to theft, and Percy was inclined to believe him. They moved to the rear of the barn and did what they could to bring comfort and reassurance to a tearful, moaning Martha.

When the doctor finally arrived, accompanied by Colonel Channing and his wife, and a kitchen maid carrying a bowl of hot water and towels, Percy and Jack made their excuses and left, assuring the Colonel that neither of their unwanted guests had been guilty of any offence, and requesting that they be dealt with in a kindly way, given the season of the year. Then it was back into the coach and the delayed trip to Tanner's Antiques.

Jack was more than a little underwhelmed by Percy's reaction to the Christmas present for Esther that he was so proud of having located. Far from congratulating his nephew on his success and perseverance, Percy seemed more interested in a large oil painting that depicted a scene in the Scottish Highlands, complete with longhorn cattle looking disapprovingly at the artist.

'That's a Millais, isn't it?' Percy said, to Jack's total amazement.

The proprietor smiled condescendingly. 'Sir obviously has an artistic eye, but I'm afraid that particular painting was purchased only this morning, by a gentleman from Mayfair. That's in London,' he added for effect.

'Is it the original?' Percy enquired with apparent indifference.

The proprietor nodded. 'Of course — there are no imitations in this establishment.'

Percy suddenly seemed to realise that time was slipping away and he hastily extracted his cheque book and paid for Jack's purchase, then advised the proprietor that he'd be sending his own private carrier to collect it.

Outside the shop, Jack was annoyed. 'I bet if we went back in there, you wouldn't even be able to identify what we just bought,' he complained as he scuttled after his swiftly striding uncle.

'Which way is the Post Office?' Percy demanded by way of response.

'Back up to the main street, then left,' Jack told him. 'But why?'

'Because they're bound to have a telephone, and I need to contact the Yard urgently.'

'Am I allowed to know why?' Jack persevered.

Percy grinned. 'Because my Christmas present arrived early. Unless I'm very much mistaken, that oil painting and some vases I noticed in the shop were until very recently in the Belgravia drawing room of the Foreign Secretary. By the close of business today, that snooty antique dealer will be reassessing his Christmas holiday.'

'Don't tell me that Esther's present was stolen property?'

'I don't remember it being on the list I was given, but I post-dated my cheque, just in case.'

Two hours later, Mr Augustus Tanner had been taken away in manacles in the back of a Scotland Yard paddy wagon, Percy had told a relieved Jack that the wall cabinet with inlaid sewing machine had not been stolen — or, at least, it was not on Percy's list — and a local carrier had been commissioned to convey it to the Enright house in Church Lane, Barking. The only cause for regret was that for the remainder of that afternoon, before Jack waved Percy farewell on the departing train for Liverpool Street, his uncle insisted on humming what he claimed was the tune to 'God Rest Ye, Merry Gentlemen'.

A week later, on Christmas morning, the Reverend Nicholas Spendlove beamed down at the full pews below his raised pulpit as the service was drawing to a close and announced that the members of the Sunday School congregation would now present the Nativity that they had spent the past three months rehearsing under the tireless supervision of their Superintendent, Millicent Frobisher.

Esther Enright smiled lovingly, and Jack held his breath apprehensively, as Lily wobbled into view from the choir stalls in the costume that Esther had consigned so much care and devotion into — her angel's wings shimmering in the gas lighting that was needed on that sullenly overcast day.

Without once pausing or losing her place, Lily discharged her duties as the 'Angel of the Lord' bringing the good word to 'certain poor shepherds' abiding on the floor in front of the first pew, one of whom was Bertie, chafing reluctantly from behind his scratchy false beard.

Two hours later, they were all seated around Constance's dining table and Percy was rubbing his hands together gleefully before being reminded by Aunt Beattie that three helpings of plum pudding would be a mortal sin. He was well into his second, and gathering his arguments together for a third, when Constance announced that they'd all be attending Evensong before supper, at the special request of the Reverend Spendlove. The children were excused when they promised to play nicely with their new toys under Cook's supervision, and it was left to an indignant Percy to act as spokesman for the adults as he demanded to know why.

'Didn't we do our bit this morning?' he whined. 'And surely God won't miss us just this once? If He really is the one from whom all blessings flow at this time of the year, then He'll surely be too exhausted to notice our absence.'

'I don't know why the vicar particularly asked for the attendance this evening of an incorrigible old blasphemer like you,' Constance replied icily, 'but the fact remains that he did. You and Jackson, seemingly. And you'll get no supper until you do.'

'After what he's eaten for dinner,' Beattie chimed in resignedly, 'there'd be no room anyway. Perhaps as well — after mince pies, Percy turns into a flatulence factory.'

As the Enrights sat, still digesting their enormous dinner at shortly after seven o'clock that evening, the vicar stepped into his pulpit and looked out at his much smaller evening congregation with an expression of suppressed awe.

'As most of you will recall with loving pride,' he began, 'the children of our Sunday School treated us to the traditional Nativity earlier on this most joyful of days in the Christian calendar. But this evening I can bring even more joyous news, of a real Nativity much closer to our humble parish. Earlier this week, not too far from here, a young couple sought refuge from the elements in a stable not unlike the one in which Christ was born. They were homeless, and the woman, whose name is Martha, was, like the Biblical Mary, expecting their first child. Believe it or not, the father is named Joseph, and he is a carpenter by trade. In attendance were three farmhands, not dissimilar to the shepherds we hear of in the Gospel of Luke.

'The child was delivered without harm and it is a boy, whom they have chosen to call "Peter". They are now happily housed and looking forward to a much happier future, thanks — perhaps unbelievably — to three wise men. The first was the doctor who delivered the infant. The second is Colonel Channing, on whose property he was born, and who — along with his gracious wife — has offered them all a home and work on his estate. But the final wise man — or, more precisely, men — are in the congregation this evening.'

Jack and Percy shuffled with embarrassment as the vicar continued.

'I refer to Jackson Enright and his uncle, Percy Enright, both of whom serve the community selflessly as police officers. They were the first on the scene, and they ensured that the appropriate medical assistance was summoned, and that the couple and their child were afforded every kindness. And so we thank them for epitomising the spirit of this holy day of Christ's birth, and ask God to bring down His boundless blessings upon them.'

A still red-faced Jack was embraced and kissed passionately by Esther as soon as they were stood back out in the entrance porch of St Margaret's.

'You're a dead loss sometimes, Jack Enright,' she whispered, 'but you're also the best man I ever met, and I thank God every day for bringing us together.'

A further embarrassed Percy looked up at the heavy snowflakes that were swirling into the porch on a persistent easterly wind. 'Good to know that it worked out all right for them in the end. Let us pray that God's boundless blessings come in the form of mince pies.'

'And that He sends down His blessed mercies for those who have to share a bed with you afterwards,' Beattie added starchily.

Percy chuckled. 'All part of the package you signed up for, my dear. But all in all, this has turned into a wonderful Christmas. Is it too early to order another one for next year?'

Want more adventures with the Enright family?
Start reading the Esther and Jack Enright Mystery series now!

Connect with David Field!
Facebook/DavidFieldAuthor
Twitter: @DavidFi32735940
davidfieldauthor.com

SECRET SANTA BY KIM FLEET

Cheltenham, England, 2015

'Merry bloody Christmas,' Private Investigator Eden Grey muttered to herself as she drew back her curtains and looked out over the rain-sodden Cheltenham rooftops. She had gone down with flu on the 19th December, and it was only now, on the 27th, having spent a wretched Christmas, that she was starting to feel vaguely human again.

As she turned away from the window, she noticed a white triangle poking underneath her front door and bent to retrieve an envelope from the floor. 'Miss Grey' was inscribed in a quavering hand across the front. Inside was small sheet of thick cream writing paper bearing a single sentence: *Who is following me?*

Eden's mind quickened as she turned the paper over. Handwritten and shoved under her door — it was most likely one of the other residents of the Art Deco block of flats she called home. The writing was thin and spidery, suggesting an elderly person. But why not just make an appointment, state the problem, and hire her PI services in the usual way? Eden scrunched up the note and her hand hovered over the recycling bin. Then again, she had nothing else better to do and it would at least keep her skills sharp.

She positioned herself on her balcony with a pair of binoculars and her phone set to voice activated recording. Mummified in two thick sweaters, a long wool coat, scarf, gloves and hat, she was toasty but barely able to move. From her eyrie she commanded a view of the car park in front of the flats, the large cedar tree in the middle of the lawn, and the road beyond.

'Ten twenty-three, young couple, matching red anoraks, leave building,' Eden said into the phone, scanning the street as the couple headed towards town. 'Nothing. Male, black jeans, black hoodie pulled over his face, pavement opposite. Now gone.' A moment later she added, 'Ten thirty-one, same male back again, waiting on the corner.'

Heels rapped on the tarmac below.

'Ten thirty-one, elderly woman, purple wool coat, black hat, gloves and handbag, walking stick, leaves building.'

Eden tracked the woman down the drive. As she turned right and headed towards the university, the man in black peeled away from the wall. Eden followed him with the binoculars, noting how he clipped his stride to match the old woman's and how he remained on the opposite pavement. She lost them at the corner, but two minutes later the woman returned and shortly afterwards the man slunk past the flats and got into a blue Honda parked on the street. The car did not leave.

Inside her building, the lift hummed up to the top floor. Eden kept watch over the man in the Honda and when an hour later she heard the lift being summoned, she slunk out and made her way downstairs as swiftly as her still-wobbly legs allowed. She hunkered down inside her car when the woman emerged, got into an A2B taxi and headed towards town. Immediately, as the taxi went past, the Honda slid out. Eden waited until two cars passed, then she too joined the parade.

The Honda clung to the taxi's rear bumper. He was evidently a rookie. Some of the tension in Eden's chest released; she wasn't dealing with a pro. She revised that opinion when the taxi drew up outside the library, the woman slowly climbed out, thanked the driver, and took her time about wriggling her fingers into her gloves and setting her handbag in the crook of her elbow. There was the merest flicker, a barely detectable widening of the eyes before the woman walked on.

Eden froze. She knew that technique of widening the field of vision to check for surveillance without anyone realising what you were doing. Eden had been taught it in her undercover days. The question was, how did this prim old woman know it?

The woman entered the library, left after fifteen minutes, and went into a café. She selected a seat at the back, commanding views of the street and the whole café, and extracted a book of crosswords from her bag. She appeared to be engrossed in her puzzle, but tiny muscle movements signalled to Eden she had the whole café tapped. The man in black slunk into a café across the street and took up residence in the window, where he remained until the woman left.

The man didn't follow the woman home but drove through Cheltenham and out along the Golden Valley to the outskirts of Gloucester. He parked in front of a long-stay hotel and went inside. Eden waited until a light went on upstairs, then counted the windows: two up, three along. Suddenly crushed by post-flu fatigue, she called it a day and drove home.

The blue Honda was back in position by nine o'clock the next morning. This time, when the old woman left with the Honda in pursuit, Eden took the lift to the top floor. Two blank-faced doors met her, offering no clues as to which was the old woman's. While she dithered, one of the doors opened and a man in his forties emerged.

'You're that PI, aren't you?' he greeted her. 'Investigating the burglary?'

Burglary? 'Yes — what do you know about it?' Eden adlibbed.

He pointed to the other door. 'Last Wednesday I heard a funny noise, so I came out to see what was going on. There was a man acting odd.'

'What was he doing?'

'He'd got a great big bunch of keys and was trying them in the lock one by one, then shoving the door with his shoulder.'

'Get a look at him?'

'Not what I was expecting,' the man admitted. 'Grey hair, thin. I asked him what he was doing. He said he was from A2B taxis and was collecting Marion for a hospital appointment. I told him to sling his hook.' Eden doubted it was phrased quite that way. 'Marion went white when I told her what had happened.'

Eden ran her fingers over the door and lock. The frame was sturdy, but there were scratches on the metal lock and the wood around it. A botch job. 'Have you made a statement to the police?' she asked.

'She hasn't reported it.' He grinned at her. 'Got you now, though, hasn't she?'

She has indeed, Eden thought. *Time to find out more about this incompetent burglar.* Pausing only to collect her picklocks, a baseball cap and a large brown envelope, she returned to the low rent hotel in Gloucester.

A neon sign announcing the Glevum Hotel stood sentry over the entrance to the carpark. Cut-price Las Vegas. Some of the letters had blown and the sign read Glum Hel. Eden tugged the baseball cap down over her hair and ran her tongue over the gummed envelope flap, sticking it down. She scrawled *Mr John Smith* across the front.

A burly man with a record-breaking beard stepped out just as she approached the front door.

'Hold the door for us, mate,' she called. When he hesitated, she flapped the envelope. 'Serving papers.'

'Someone in trouble?' *Is it me?* was written all over his face.

'Divorce, by the look of it,' she said, heading inside and calling over her shoulder. 'Always at Christmas, eh?'

The lobby smelled of microwave pies and despair. The residents of Glum Hel were most likely separated, laid off, or working homeless. People like her, delivering bad news, would not be a novelty. As if to confirm that life was truly unkind, the carpet was a 1970s brown and gold headache. Above, the ceiling bore a death-trap layer of polystyrene tiles.

The stair carpet was a dizzying excess in pinks and greens, patched with crosses of gaffer tape. Eden trotted up to the landing, turned left and walked to the end of the corridor, then returned, counting the doors. At the third, she stopped and listened. To the right, silence; to the left, a TV show about buying crap at boot sales.

For form's sake, she knocked on the door, waited for ten seconds, then slid her picklocks out of her pocket and set to work. Security, like safety, was slack at Glum Hel, and the door knob turned after only a few seconds' work.

Eden stepped inside quickly. The room was small and square with a shower cubicle in one corner that lent a musty smell. The bed was neatly made and a few clothes hung tidily on a rail. Underneath the window was a table covered with photographs of the old woman, laid out like a mosaic. Different clothes, different light levels; these had been taken over a period of days, and throughout the whole day. Whoever he was, he meant business.

She dug out her phone and snapped the layout on the table. Just as she reached the door to leave, it opened, stubbing against her toe. The man in black lunged at her, knocking her off balance. She threw out her arm and landed heavily on it, then sprang to her feet and charged at the man, hurtling him towards the door. The door handle jabbed hard into his kidneys. His knees buckled and he fought for breath. She hauled him to his feet and pushed him into a chair.

'Burglary's illegal you know,' the man rasped.

'So's stalking.' That brief scuffle had knocked the stuffing out of Eden. Pain shot up her arm from her wrist to her shoulder. 'Who are you and what are you up to?'

'I could ask you the same thing.'

She flashed her private investigator's ID, and the man crumpled like an over-whisked meringue. He was about seventy, with deep life-weary lines scoring his face, and his clothes hung loosely on his angular frame. Not her usual nemesis.

'My name is Martin Collins,' the man said. 'She is Marion Greatorex, and she's my mother.' He looked up at her with cloudy blue eyes.

Whatever scenarios Eden had entertained when she started this assignment, it wasn't that. Eventually she echoed, 'Your mother?'

'She abandoned me in the hospital where I was born when I was a few hours old.'

Martin rose and fetched a scrapbook from the bedside table. Eden flipped through the pages. The first held a printout of a newspaper article dated March 1946, calling for Marion Lovell to come forwards as there were fears for her welfare. She was described as aged twenty-three, with dark hair and a large scar on her left arm. A photograph of the baby she left behind dominated the page.

'When I was eighteen, my parents told me I was adopted, and since then I've wondered who I really am. Just before she died, my adoptive mother told me I was abandoned. That was ten years ago. I've been looking for Marion Lovell ever since.'

'How did you find her?'

'I trawled online and searched the birth, marriage and death records,' Martin said. 'She married and became Marion Greatorex. I put out an appeal on Facebook and someone came forwards.' He turned to a page in the scrapbook and Eden read an email from a former pupil at the Cheltenham Ladies College: *We all loved Mrs Greatorex. She taught French and was always thinking up fun ways for us to practise our vocab. Yes, she did have a scar. She usually wore long sleeves but one sports day she took off her cardigan and there it was. A pan of hot milk, she said.*

'What are you going to do?' Eden asked.

Martin twisted his fingers together. 'I meant to confront her, but when it came to it, I didn't have the bottle.' His eyes met hers. 'What if she denied it? Me.' He glanced away again. 'I've only got this room for another couple of days, and I doubt I'll be back.'

'You live a long way away?'

'It's not that. I don't have long left.'

Now Eden looked closely at him, she saw his yellowed eyes and pouchy, jaundiced skin. 'Why did you try to break into her flat?'

Martin flushed. 'I was hoping she'd kept something of me.' He shrugged. 'A baby's toy, a hospital bracelet. And I half-hoped she'd discover me in the act and it would all come out.'

Deep sadness washed over Eden at the desperation on his face. 'Let me speak to her, see what she says,' she said. As she stood to go, she added, 'And stop following her.'

In her car, Eden lolled against the seat, lightheaded with fatigue. Every muscle in her body screamed, and a headache pounded the top of her skull. The traffic was just starting to clot. With luck she could make it home before the Golden Valley snarled with commuters.

She was out of luck, and it was a tortuous forty-five minute journey to her flat. Glancing up, she saw a light behind the curtains that shrouded Marion Greatorex's life. Despite her brain fog, her mind buzzed. Who was this woman who practised deep-cover tradecraft, why had she abandoned her baby, and why didn't she report the attempted burglary to the police?

Inside, Eden ran a hot bath and dumped in a generous serving of lemon and bergamot bath salts. Thinking time. Submerged like a hippo, with only her eyes above the surface of the water, Eden reviewed what she knew about her mysterious client. If she was twenty-three in 1946, Marion was now ninety-two. Sprightly, lived alone. A former teacher. Maybe that was a good place to start.

An internet search revealed an old girls' association, and Eden tapped out a general request for anyone who remembered Marion Greatorex *née* Lovell to get in touch.

The next morning, a reply from a former teacher was waiting in her inbox. Crossing her fingers, Eden rang her and said she was writing a book about inspirational teachers. They arranged to meet in the coffee lounge at the Imperial Hotel.

Clara Hoskins was small, blonde and bird-like, with bright all-seeing eyes and quick movements. She ordered hot chocolate and a slice of fruit cake and sat forwards in her chair, eager to begin in a way that Eden found endearing. If only everyone she questioned could be so accommodating.

'You worked with Marion Greatorex?' Eden began.

'She was a few years ahead of me,' Clara blurted out, almost before Eden finished the question. 'I started in 1958, and

Marion had been there a decade already. She was French and Games; I was History. Though of course after a while she dropped the Games.' She paused for breath and to take a bite of fruitcake.

Eden seized the opportunity to ask, 'Did you know her before she was married?'

'She married awfully late. A sweetheart killed in the war, and after that no one was quite up to snuff. Until she met Cyril, of course. He was Scotch. Got married in a kilt!'

'You went to the wedding?'

'No. Though we all chipped in for a super present. Spode tea set? Can't remember now, but it would have been good because we all adored her.'

'But you didn't go to the wedding?'

Clara shook her head. 'A very small do. They were both quite old for a first marriage. I think that's why it was just them, his brother and her mother. Both his parents and her father were dead. So sad. They married on the day Neil Armstrong walked on the moon, so they missed that! Though I don't suppose they minded a bit.'

Eden's hand cramped as she tried to jot it all down. 'What did she do before she came to Cheltenham Ladies?'

Clara scrunched up her face to assist her memory. 'During the war she was in an office. Something boring, she said, at The Ministry of Agriculture and Fisheries.'

Eden glanced up from her notepad. 'And after the war?'

'Teacher training, I suppose.' Clara eulogised for some time about how the girls loved Marion Greatorex, then suddenly swooped into her bag and produced a photograph. 'Here's me and Marion at sports day not long after I started at the school,' she said.

Eden took the photograph. It showed a young, fresh-faced woman in a short tennis skirt standing next to a smiling older woman, their blonde heads tilted towards each other. Friends. Eden took a copy on her phone and returned it.

Back in her flat, Eden made a pot of coffee, spread a large sheet of paper across her table and assembled the facts. In the centre she placed the original note, *Who is following me?* The letters were strangely formed. Not an English hand, she thought. She frowned at it for a while then pressed speed dial on her phone. Time to call in reinforcements.

After a dozen rings, her friend Judy's voice came on the line. Screams and crashes echoed in the background, and a child's voice whined repeatedly, 'It's my turn.'

'Can I borrow Marcus?' Marcus was Judy's long-suffering husband.

'How long for? A year, two, a decade? Would you like a child or three as well? Take as many as you like.'

'Marcus for two hours would be fine.'

'You can come round now,' Judy said, 'as long as you bring any leftover choccies.'

'Deal.'

Judy's house was a Victorian semi near the station. Silver strands of tinsel dripped from an olive tree in a pot by the door and tangled in the cotoneaster hedge flanking the front wall. Judy flung open the door before Eden had knocked and hustled her into the cosy chaos she loved. As she entered, Eden trod on a plastic brick and pain shot through her foot.

'Thanks for the present,' one of Judy's sons told Eden solemnly as she hopped on one leg. The remains of the building set she'd given them were scattered across the rug.

'You're welcome,' Eden grimaced.

'You want my help?' Marcus asked. He was a quiet, shy man completely overshadowed by the statuesque Judy.

'You do family history research, don't you?' Eden said. 'Can you help me find someone?'

'We can give it a go.' He ushered her into the dining room, where a laptop stood open on the table. A jiggle of the mouse brought it to life.

Judy plonked herself on one side of Marcus, Eden on the other, the three of them fencing elbows.

'I want to find out more about this woman, Marion Greatorex,' Eden said. 'Where she came from, who her family are.' *Who she really is.*

'What do you know already?'

'Born around 1923, maiden name Lovell, married in 1969 to Cyril Greatorex.'

Marcus opened up a genealogy site and tapped in a few details. 'Hm. A few possibles for him on the 1939 census. Is she still alive?'

'Very much so.'

'Then she'll be redacted.' Marcus muttered to himself and logged into another website. While he typed in names and dates, Eden handed Judy the note.

'What do you make of this?'

'That's it?' Judy said. 'Not much to go on.'

'What about the writing itself?'

'Old, probably a woman. Froggy.'

'French? Not German?'

'No. It looks exactly like my old French teacher's writing. "Judy, not good enough, see me after class." Old bat.'

'You sure the marriage was 1969?' Marcus asked.

'The same day as the moon landing,' Eden said.

'Let's try a wildcard. There she is.'

Eden and Judy leaned forwards. 'Can you find a birth certificate?' Eden asked.

'We'd need to know where she was born,' Marcus said, 'but that'll be on the marriage certificate.'

'And the birth certificate will give me her parents' names?'

'Only her father.' Marcus clicked the mouse a couple of times. 'Want me to order a copy for you?'

'Marcus!' Judy rolled her eyes at his idiocy. 'As if you need to ask.'

Marcus arranged for an express delivery and the certificate arrived the next day. Eden tore it open with shaking fingers. Marion's full name was given as Marion Aimée Lovell, schoolteacher, born in London. Her father was Gerald Lovell, deceased.

Eden sighed and rubbed her eyes. She was not much further forwards. She'd have to get Marcus to try to find the birth certificate. Her gaze travelled down the certificate to the witnesses — Patrick Greatorex and Aimée Durant Lovell. What had Clara told her? The only people at the wedding were the groom's brother and the bride's mother. They must be the witnesses. Aimée Durant. She'd bet Marion learned her French hand at her mother's knee.

Eden powered up her laptop and opened a search engine. Searches on 'Marion Lovell', 'Marion Greatorex' and 'Marion Durant' returned nothing. On a hunch, she tried 'Marianne Durant' and struck gold — a 'Where are they now?' article that told her exactly why her upstairs neighbour didn't want to draw attention to herself.

Gathering her papers into a cardboard file, Eden toiled up the stairs and rang the bell.

'You were quicker than I thought you'd be,' Marion greeted her. She showed Eden into a neat sitting room with a plum-coloured plush suite and coal-effect electric fire. 'You've found him?'

'His name is Martin Collins and he thinks you're his mother,' Eden said.

'Nonsense, I can't … couldn't…'

'I know,' Eden said, and repeated what Martin had told her. 'The woman who gave birth to him said her name was Marion Lovell. She had a scar on her left arm, the same scar you have, but unlike her you have blonde hair. Martin's mother was a brunette.'

'Who could it…?' Marion lapsed into thought, and after a few seconds whispered, 'Martine.'

'You were afraid he was digging into your past, trying to find out who you really are, weren't you?' Eden said. 'When I was watching him following you, I noticed you have certain skills you didn't acquire as a French teacher, nor at The Ministry of Agriculture. It's a shame the Ministry cover story has been aired in certain documentaries about the war.'

Marion tilted her chin, and Eden saw the brave, ruthless young woman she had been.

'You have my word that I will never reveal your secret,' Eden said. 'There's a woman looking for the last remaining members of the Special Operations Executive believed to have survived the war. One of those people is Marianne Durant. That's you, isn't it?'

Marion stared into the fire. 'Even my husband never knew,' she said.

'Who is the woman who pretended to be you? Martin's mother?'

'It can only be Martine Fournier. We worked together during the war. She allowed herself to be captured by German soldiers so I could get away. I was able to warn the others and they escaped. Three weeks later, I was captured and sent to Ravensbrück. Martine was there. We knew we would probably die, so we told each other all about our real lives. It was comforting to know there was ordinariness still going on in the world, despite the horror.' Marion visibly composed herself. 'Whiskey?'

'Please.'

Marion poured generous slugs into two crystal tumblers and lifted her glass. 'To you and Martine, wherever she is.' She drank deeply. 'I imagine the boy wasn't conceived in the best of ways. She probably assumed I was dead and borrowed my name. I owed her my life.'

'The identical scars?'

'We were tattooed by the guards. Impossible to get it removed by a doctor — too many awkward questions. I don't know how she did hers, but I got rid of mine with acid.'

Eden could barely imagine the danger and pain this woman endured for her country. 'Why me?' she asked at last.

Bright eyes appraised her. 'You check under your car every time you get in it, you seal your flat so you know if anyone searches it, and you are constantly alert,' she said. 'As you pointed out, it takes one to know one. I noticed you'd been rather poorly-looking and alone this Christmas, and I thought a mystery would perk you up. A gift, if you like, from one spook to another.'

'A secret Santa,' Eden said. 'Thank you, it did the trick.'

'This Martin Collins,' Marion said. 'How long has he got?'

'Months, maybe.'

Marion fixed her gaze on the window, where a chill end-of-year sunshine braved the bone-cold sky. 'Martine pretended to be me; I can pretend to be her. After all, being someone else is what we're trained to do, isn't it, Eden?'

Eden thought of her old life, the one she'd been forced to leave behind, and nodded.

'Come and see me again,' Marion said. 'I have stories I think you'll enjoy and no one else to share them with.'

'It's a date,' Eden said, and went to phone Martin to tell him his mother wanted to see him.

Want to uncover more secrets with Eden?
Read the first book in the Eden Grey Mystery Series now!

Connect with Kim Fleet!
Facebook/KimFleetWriter
Twitter: @KimFleet
www.kimfleet.com

STIR UP SUNDAY BY M J LOGUE

London, 1665

'You want me to what?' Major Thankful Russell said blankly.

King Charles II's spymaster, Thomas Killigrew, pirouetted. Killigrew probably didn't mean to spin like a top, but he was in a towering temper, and — regrettably, for a man attempting to invoke fear and trembling — equally towering heels. When not being a spymaster and courtier, Master Killigrew was also theatre manager to the King's Company. It explained a lot about his sartorial excesses. He pursed his lips irritably. 'Find that book.'

'That's what I thought you said.'

Killigrew never dealt well with Russell's habitual lack of due deference. He stiffened so abruptly that his borrowed curls quivered. 'Are you grown deaf, as well as —'

'Don't talk to my husband like that in his own house,' Thomazine Russell said silkily. Her cheeks were almost as red as her hair, and her husband wondered quite how much of the previous exchange she'd overheard. 'It's snowing quite heavily, Master Killigrew. I shouldn't like you to spoil your —' Thomazine's eyes rested on his feet — 'lovely shoes, now, if any more should settle.'

Killigrew was also notoriously single-minded. 'That book must go to print by Christmas, sir. Why, we shall ensure that your bewitching little minx has her own copy, hot from the press!'

'Don't try too hard,' Thomazine murmured, for her husband's ears only, and then, louder, 'I don't care to be described as either bewitching or a minx, by a man to whom I have no ties of affection.'

'Ah, I forgot from what outspoken roots you sprang!' Killigrew smiled — it probably worked on actresses — and winked roguishly. 'Such a spitfire! — but then, what else would suit you, you old firebrand?' he said, turning to Russell. It wasn't a question either were willing to answer, so the spymaster slapped his gloves into his palm, equilibrium quite restored. 'Splendid! I'll tell His Majesty you'll see his manuscript returned to the sign of the Weeping Angel by Christmas Eve.'

'His Majesty — what?'

Thomazine might as well not have spoken. Since Master Killigrew didn't acknowledge women unless he was engaged in active congress with them, it fell to her husband to ask, 'What does His Majesty have to do with stolen recipe books?'

'Major Russell, sir, you have not been paying attention! The book — do keep up — you might say is a pet project of His Majesty's. A little whimsy.'

'I had not realised His Majesty's literary ambitions extended to plum-pudding,' he murmured.

Thomazine snorted and Killigrew shot her a look of loathing.

'A whimsy,' the little man repeated grimly. 'The Muse called, and His Majesty answered. Well, he means to see that manuscript in print, Major, and I mean you to retrieve it. Since it was likely one of your sort that stole it in the first place, you can doubtless walk into whatever nasty little republican nest of vipers you presently grace with your company, and ask for it back.'

'It's a coffee-house.' He had been dealing with Killigrew's flouncing for some years now. It amused Thomazine, and it amused Russell to amuse his wife. 'They don't serve vipers.'

'You are being obtuse, sir.' Under the mannered waves of somebody else's hair, the little spymaster blinked once, slowly, like a lizard. 'That is a direction.'

When you dealt with affected theatrical hangers-on professionally on a daily basis, you grew to understand that the words mattered. It was a direction from on high, then, not open to negotiation. Russell tucked his hair — his own hair: Killigrew hated that — behind his ears and sighed. 'By Christmas Eve.'

'It is a gift for Her Majesty.' Now that he was getting his own way, the fussy little man was all sweetness and light again. 'Who knows, perhaps we could see our way to a little Christmas gift for your own queen?'

'We are a decent household,' Thomazine said, straight-faced. 'We don't keep Christmas in this house. And we don't hold with queens.'

That choked Killigrew off. There was nothing he could say to a good Puritan housewife, and so he said nothing — which was a crowning mercy — and stalked down the stairs without mincing once.

'How do you not kill him?' she asked, once the street door had banged shut after him.

'Self-discipline, tibber.' Her husband leaned on the windowsill and watched the snow falling. It almost managed to make Aldgate beautiful, which took some doing. It wasn't the loveliest or quietest part of London, but Russell was fond of it. Every one of these streets had a kind memory. They had spent the first weeks of their married life here, and it had been a very heaven — when they weren't being shot at, chased by murderers and accused of treason, at any rate. Not that they'd been married for that long, either. Long enough to not mind the being shot at, chased by murderers and accused of treason, so long as they were in each other's company.

He turned around, preparing to be stern. 'I wish you hadn't lied, though.'

She gave him her wicked, loving smile. 'It was that or hit him with something heavy. And it shifted him.'

'Yes, but —'

She stood on tiptoe and kissed him. 'Of course we'll keep Christmas — I only said that to frighten him off.' And then she put her arms round him, tucking her head under his chin in the most confiding way. 'Anyway, I didn't lie. We'll be back home by then, so technically, we won't be celebrating Christmas in this house.'

'Provided it doesn't keep snowing.'

'Oh, we'll find a way.'

It was a thing he loved about his wife. He fretted and complicated, but she simply rolled up her sleeves and set to work cheerfully. She was a wonderfully wise, pragmatic, unstoppable force of nature — she had been determined to leave their baby half a day's ride hence in Buckinghamshire whilst they packed up the last of the house in Aldgate, preferring to leave the boy with a wet-nurse than expose him to the stench of London — but there were times when he could wish she was slightly more biddable.

'It will be fine,' Thomazine said, smiling up at him. 'Tell me of this recipe book, then.'

'It's not a real recipe book — which might be useful. It's a nasty parcel of hyperbole written by a man wishing to elicit laughter at another's expense, to make himself appear wittier than he is.'

'Good lord, husband. You're grown all Parliamentarian on me again.'

'Possibly because His Majesty is grown all tyrannical on me, tibber. A cruel joke against the Cromwells. The joke is that not only was the late Lord Protector a wrong 'un, but that his wife was a nasty slattern, much above herself, who left a deal to be desired in the decency department. Imagine a real queen, writing out recipes and household economies?'

'The King wrote that?' Even in the kind firelight, her face had whitened, dark stripes on her cheeks as if he'd physically slapped her.

Russell nodded. 'Did you think he was no more than a genial philanderer, love? I suspect he has a deep capacity for hate, that one. Even now. There are times when he bothers me.'

'Enough to have him beheaded?' she said warily.

He grinned. 'No, tibber. It caused enough bother when we removed the present incumbent's father, and I'm too old and set in my ways to go through all that again. This one can keep his head on his shoulders, though I might wish he used it for something kinder than thinking up ways to abuse poor Mistress Cromwell for the amusement of his cronies.'

Thomazine untwined her arms from him, stepping back abruptly. 'But you're not going to let it be printed … are you?'

'Do I have a choice, tibber? I'm ordered, remember.'

'But —'

'Another of His Majesty's whimsies. Being the most conspicuous old Roundhead in his intelligence service, I'm the most likely candidate to deal with subversive thievery. And a reminder that I may enjoy some degree of Royal toleration, but I'm still considered a whisker away from outright treason.'

'But she's a harmless old lady. Why would you hurt her?' Suddenly her eyes were brimming with tears, which he could not bear.

He took her hands in his. 'It's a stupid pamphlet, of no accounting —'

'Calling a decent woman names? It is not of no account, Russell, that's how women are judged, that is who we are!' She was weeping in earnest now. 'Talking about her — and her husband, she married him freely — as if they're no more than pieces of wood! She is a thinking, feeling person and that man is writing calumny about her as if she doesn't matter, and people will remember that about her forever!'

'Oh, love —'

'Imagine if I had lost you, but must listen to people say how evil you were and how you deserved to be dead? Calling me a bad mother, and an upstart slut — it all a great jest to the world, and me not able to answer it? Russell, you can't get that horrible thing back! You can't do that to her!'

Thankful Russell had known Oliver Cromwell, in another life. He didn't think the late Lord Protector had ever cared what the world called him so long as he'd done right by his conscience. But he'd known the man's wife, briefly, too. And she cared, very much, what the neighbours thought.

He sighed. 'Well, it would seem we must still find the damned thing, if only to be sure no other bugger prints it, either.'

'I don't know where it is,' the proprietor of the Weeping Angel snarled. 'I left it here, ready for the devil to fetch the type. Was just before we locked up the night afore last, and it's disappeared!' He glowered at Thomazine. 'And what the hell d'you bring her in here for?'

It was likely that the angel after whom this printing establishment was named had wept at Nathaniel Goodbody's housekeeping. There was a particular smell attached to printer's establishments. A year ago, it would have had Thomazine heaving up her breakfast over the jumbled rows of leaden letters. Now it only made her nose twitch. Even so, even with the draught from the neatly-stuffed window over the press, she had to swallow a few times. 'Have you checked the floor?' she said — she couldn't help it — 'everything else seems to be kept there?'

'Did you bring her only to criticise my cleanliness, sir?'

'Oh no,' Russell said in his mildest voice, 'she acts as a restraint. I bite, else.' He gave a faint smile. 'Tell me about the manuscript, sir.'

'I'll wait outside,' she said. 'Since you haven't bitten anyone since breakfast, dear.'

The printer wiped his hands on his apron. 'About sixty pages, close script, demy quarto.'

'And it arrived intact?'

'It arrived,' he said grimly, 'courtesy of some ars— begging your pardon, mistress, but since you shouldn't be here anyway you shouldn't mind language — some bullet-headed thug dropped it off. Bloody docker, he was, massive feller with a great big scar on his...' his voice trailed off. Even under the greasy ink-marks, his Adam's apple bobbed as he realised just how tactless it was to talk of scars when Russell's face was so marred by his own.

'On his...?' Russell prompted, with gentle malice.

Goodbody tapped the side of his head, above his ear, nervously. 'Black as the Devil, he was, like he hadn't washed in a week. Black hair, black eyes, cropped like a convict. Ant he talked lak dis.' He affected a theatrical German accent. 'Signed my chitty R.R — Robert Rhymes, he said. The which it don't.'

Russell — tall, scarred, but with a mercifully blonde ponytail — suddenly looked as if he might laugh. Of course — Prince

Rupert of the Rhine. Running nefarious errands for his nephew, the King, whilst disguised as a docker. A man had to do something useful with his retirement, after all.

'Do you know the author personally, sir?' he said.

Goodbody shook his head. 'Fritzy there gave me gold — in advance — said he'd collect Christmas Eve. Which was sooner than is usual, but —' he rubbed thumb and forefinger together in an unmistakable gesture — 'he who pays the piper calls the tune, know what I mean? Especially when he pays the piper more'n expected. He's going to go mental when it's not ready. Sixty sovereigns is sixty sovereigns, however you slice it.'

'Could you not merely reimburse the, ah, the large German gentleman, when he calls for his pamphlets? And say you were unable to accommodate him?'

'I haven't got it,' Goodbody muttered. 'I spent it.' He shifted some letters about awkwardly. 'I give the 'prentices a few shillings extra for Christmas, all right? Bought the wife a new frock — she hasn't had one since our Toby was born, thought it be nice for her to look pretty for church on Christmas morning — and I paid the rent on this place for the last quarter, what was becoming pressing to the point of eviction; you want to see the bleedin' receipt for it or what?'

Russell put his head on one side and said, 'Yes, I rather think I do.'

The snow was settling thickly, which was a mercy because Thomazine suspected that which lay in the alley at the side of the Weeping Angel might be yellow, otherwise.

There was a small dog rooting in the drifts, digging up rubbishy wet papers with its front paws. It looked up at her jealously and growled, backing away with something clenched in its teeth. Something grey, and slender —

150

'Drop that you bugger!'

She lunged at the dog; practice made her more than a match for the horrible little terrier-thing, and her foot blocked its exit at the same time as she gripped its collar, her free hand grabbing for the draggled glove in its mouth.

'Six shillings they cost!'

It was a brief, fierce tussle. It ended in one agonised yelp from the cur, an unfeminine howl of triumph from Thomazine, and an anguished yell from the lengthening shadows of the alley. 'Leave my dog alone, missus!'

'Get your dog to leave my husband's gloves alone!' she yelled back. This was Fleet Street after all, where men were expected to roister and women were expected to be low. She hated to disappoint. 'What in God's name are you doing out here in this weather? Come here!'

He was not an ill-grown lad, or an ill-nourished one, though more than usually filthy — no, not filthy: covered in ink. 'So you're the devil,' she said, blinking.

He gave her a neat bow, grinning. Even his gums were black, which made his teeth rather alarmingly white. 'I ent that wicked, missus. Bartholomew Ward, as is 'prentice to Master Goodbody. At your service.'

Thomazine looked at him, and the grinning dog. At the broken window behind his head, and the sodden shreds of smeared paper on paws and fingers. 'I see,' she said, in a different voice altogether. 'I see.'

He stared at her guiltily. Then his gaze slid over her shoulder, widening in horror. 'I never done nuffink, missus!'

She glanced behind her. (She didn't think she would ever overlook people's horrid reactions to her husband's poor ragged cheek. More than anything, it was just rude.) 'I found the printer's devil, dear,' she told Russell — adding, just out of spite, 'He was the last person to see the manuscript. I imagine you'll have to ask him all kinds of searching questions.'

He looked at the boy, and the boy stared back, gulping as if he were expecting the searching to be done with red-hot irons. 'Is he known for breaking and entering?'

'He is not!' Master Goodbody said from behind them. 'He's a good boy, Major Russell — works hard, no trouble at all. There's only him and his brother. No drinking, no roistering, no wenching. If it warn't for them boys keeping in work, their poor old dad'd be turned out on the street.'

'Dear me. In my youth, printers' apprentices were known to be … revolutionary?'

'Not for years,' Goodbody said indignantly. 'All playbills and public hangings now, that's where the money is.'

'So you didn't take exception to the content of this manuscript, then?'

'I haven't read the damned thing, sir! That's his job! D'you think I have time to read every trumpery bit of writing I'm expected to put out?'

Thomazine tugged Russell's sleeve, before he could say anything else. 'Could we talk to Master Ward in the coffee-house? I'm getting cold.'

'You can't take a woman in a coffee-house!' both printer and devil howled, as one.

She shrugged. 'Apparently women aren't supposed to be in the shop either, gentlemen. Well, we have to be somewhere, don't we?'

'He took it,' Thomazine said, so soon as breakfast was brought and the aproned servant bustled out of earshot.

The boy bridled. 'I never!'

'Yes, you did. You came back after the shop was locked up, broke in through that window, and took the manuscript. And then dropped half of it on the way out.' She pushed the fresh-baked mutton pie towards him. 'Eat the pie. I'm not wasting it.'

'How on earth did you work that out, tibber?' Russell asked her.

'The dog,' she said. They both looked at her oddly. 'The dog was ferreting about in the alley — with your glove, Thankful — right underneath the window. It looked as if someone had dropped a bundle of papers and it had been snowed on overnight. Which, you know, wouldn't have been odd at all if you'd told Master Goodbody you'd found it, he being so worried. But you didn't.'

The apprentice-boy — she couldn't think of him as a devil, no matter what the proper word was, it was a horrible thing to say about a boy who wasn't more than fourteen — looked from one to another with his mouth ajar. 'You ain't a witch, are you? — with the hair, and — him?'

Russell gave his unnervingly slanted grin, and helped himself to a wedge of breakfast. 'She doesn't need witchcraft, sir. Well — is she right?'

'Oh yes,' Thomazine said. 'I saw it, Master Ward. Before you tucked it under your coat.'

There was a long silence. It was never quiet in the Rainbow coffee-house, which was a mercy: it would have been awkward, else. But the boy said nothing, and Thomazine said nothing, and Russell — who had a mouthful of pie at the time — said nothing either. It went on until Russell rested his chin in his hands and stared at the boy ominously.

'All right,' the boy yelped, 'I done it, what you going to do about it? Arrest me?'

'Why?'

'Tell you why, missus, cos it ain't bleedin' fair! And go on —' he shot his skinny wrists out — 'drag me off to Newgate, see if I care! My old man was one of ol' Cromwell's Ironsides, back in the day — got his leg took off in the service of the Parliament, and he always had a lot o' time for the old bugger —' He paused for breath and more pie. 'Speaking ill of a dead man ain't right, and what's worse, slandering his poor old goodwife as never did any harm —'

'Exactly,' Russell said.

The boy wasn't listening. He ploughed on, face alight with evangelical zeal. 'Profiteering, is what it is! Like taking the pennies off of a dead man's eyes, my old dad say — he said d'rather starve than take that dirty money —'

'So the Christmas box Master Goodbody meant to share amongst his apprentices from the bounty left by Master, um, Rhymes … you would have refused it?'

The stars faded somewhat from the boy's eyes. 'You what?'

'We have a dilemma. On one hand, one pernicious manuscript.'

'I'd rather have my ears nailed than give it back!'

'Oh, don't be so dramatic. I agree with you — both of you — the cruel thing should never see the light of day. However—'

'It ain't going to,' the boy said with satisfaction. 'My da burned it. The whole nasty parcel. Give or take them bits I dropped in the alley. He said he din't lose his leg for the Parliament just so that little scrote — saving your pardon, missus, His Majesty — could turn into his bloody father, miscalling decent folk —'

'In which case,' Russell said grimly, 'I suggest you think about how you plan to make that loss good, because this time tomorrow Prince Rupert is going to be knocking on your door asking for either the book or sixty sovereigns, cash. Which Master Goodbody has already spent. On back-rent for the print-shop.'

Suddenly all the fire had gone out of the lad. 'But my da said —'

'We are obliged to look at the greater picture: the publication of that horrible pamphlet, set against the loss of the print-shop. And your employment.'

Under the black smears, the boy's face had drained of colour. 'You threatening me?'

'No, young man. But I've known Rupert — or shall I say, Master Rhymes — for thirty years, and he is almost as vengeful as his nephew, the King. Though it's a close call. Rupert has the worse temperament, I should say. He may choose to make it personal. His Majesty simply has a long memory for a grievance.'

'And you work for these men?'

Russell grinned suddenly: the real, toothy one, not the polite one. 'No, Master Ward, I lived through the late wars, and I work to be sure they don't happen again. How's your handwriting?'

Sixty pages, close script, demy quarto size.

That was twenty pages each. Give or take the rags from the alley, which must still be copied out, though the worst of the calumnies were excised.

'Missus Cromwell never went to bed with her old man's officers!' Ward yelped, disgusted.

Russell sniffed. 'She never approached me, surely.'

The boy gaped at him. 'You? One of his —?'

'Possibly at the same time as your father,' he said dryly, '—ask him. I'm distinctive.'

Thomazine looked up from her end of the table. 'Shut up. And write. The both of you.'

They ran out of recipes around midnight. Thomazine took over dictation, and the two men simply wrote. When she ran out of culinary ideas, she went on to household recipes: to relieve biting fleas in dogs. To keep off the moth in wool. A most efficacious polish for furniture.

And then, as the clock of St Gabriel's chimed five o' clock on the morning of Christmas Eve, she scrubbed her hands over her face and said, 'I'm sorry, gentlemen. I am done. My brain is squeezed entirely dry of invention. And I shouldn't choose to rely on the last few, for accuracy.'

'Then I hope the moths eat all his royal drawers,' Ward said, throwing his pen down.

'Amen to that.' There was a streak of ink that ran from Russell's eyebrow up into his hair, where he had absent-mindedly rubbed at it. Thomazine licked her finger and cleaned it, and he was too tired to object.

'Now what?' she asked.

'Now we have to put the damned thing back.'

Not that there was anything suspicious about a weary goodwife with a basket, a stopped-out apprentice, and a small dog, scuttling along the deserted streets at coming up for dawn on Christmas Eve. A crumpled and unshaven Thankful Russell was suspicious, but fortunately most people were too busy making assumptions about the contents of the basket to notice an uncharacteristic untidiness. Thomazine and Russell stood guard on the main street whilst the boy took the basket and slid out of sight.

It seemed to take a hundred years, and judging by the grunting and scrabbling, all was not going well.

'Bugger's boarded the window up,' Ward panted, 'now what?'

Thomazine looked at her husband. He sighed. 'Must I add breaking and entering to my crimes?' And before either of them could stop him, he'd rapped on the front door of the Weeping Angel — and then again, with less toleration.

Master Goodbody came eventually, after they had been sworn at by most of the late-sleepers of Fleet Street for the noise: still in his nightshirt, looking even more bedraggled than Russell.

Who apologised, with a marked lack of sincerity, and said, 'We return your manuscript, sir.'

'Bloody hell,' Goodbody said.

'Indeed. I also have your apprentice — who has been helpfulness itself. I apologise for keeping him out overnight for questioning, sir. It seems we were mistaken.'

'Where? Who —'

'I am delighted to say, Master Goodbody, the manuscript did not go anywhere.'

Bartholomew Ward scampered past them into the acrid darkness, and started to dig in the heaped debris under the press.

'I did tell you,' Thomazine said apologetically. 'When I lose anything, the first thing my husband says is, did you look down the back of the settle?'

'Here it is, see? I seen some lads chucking snowballs about in the alley — did I not mention? Must ha' been one of them broke the window, eh? I reckon the draught must ha' blowed it all about,' Ward said, dumping the paper on the table. 'There's some bits got a bit wet, but that don't matter, I'll soon set that to rights —'

Goodbody had dismissed them from his mind. They were physically in his presence, still, but he had his manuscript and his sixty sovereigns, and he had an urgent job to do. 'Well, I'll wish you a merry Christmas, sir, you and your good lady. I'll not ask you to stop…'

'Take care of your apprentices, Master Goodbody,' Thomazine murmured, 'he will go far, that young man.'

'Unless monitored closely,' Russell murmured for her ears only.

It was almost full daylight. The sky was clear and pearly-grey, and if not quite cloudless, perhaps not as ominous as it had been.

Thomazine thought they were thinking the same thought. 'If we left now —'

'We could be home by dusk.' Russell stopped in the middle of a street that was growing to a bustle, as stalls opened. 'But not much of a Christmas, tibber. Without gifts, or —'

She stood on tiptoe and kissed him, not caring who disapproved of such unseemly public affection in the middle of Fleet Street. 'You've given us immortality, bless you. It's not every housewife can boast that her recipe for white-pot is preserved for posterity.'

She thought he was going to say something romantic. Instead he said, '…White-pot?'

She nodded.

'I may have forgotten. You need to show me again. As soon as we're home.'

Her mouth twitched in spite of her desire to be serious. She took his hand. 'And you think licking cream from a spoon is a dignified way for a grown man to behave?'

He gave her that lovely cockeyed grin. 'Perks of the cook's assistant, tibber. No?'

And hand in hand like children, they started to head back across London Bridge, through the thickening press of people and the bells that were beginning to ring out Christmas.

Want more adventures in 17th Century England?
Start reading the Thomazine and Thankful Russell
Thriller Series now!

Connect with M J Logue!
Facebook/MJLogue
Twitter:@Hollie_Babbitt
asweetdisorder.com

THE CHRISTMAS GHOST BY LINDA STRATMANN

Brighton, England, 1871

Mina Scarletti, her fragile form wrapped in layers of thick shawls and a deep soft cape, was travelling in response to an urgent message. December in Brighton meant bright chill skies and seas like glittering shards of ice with winds that tumbled waves onto the promenade. It was also the season of the carriage classes, when the great hotels were lit up so brightly they could be seen for miles. Fires blazed, tended by battalions of servants, and there were suppers, balls and receptions that went on into the small hours of the morning. Mina's small body with its twisted spine meant she did not attend such grand occasions, but in any case, she much preferred sitting cosily at home, writing stories about ghosts. Her one claim to fame was her reputation for exposing the villainy of fraudulent spirit mediums who preyed on the vulnerable bereaved.

She had not intended to go out that night, so very close to Christmas and with so much to do in preparation, most of which would fall on her tiny shoulders; but the message had been very urgent, and from a lady of importance. Mrs Calverdon was a widow of some means, who had once been very prominent in Brighton society. In recent years however, she had declined to go about, and was thought of as a recluse. When Mina had received the summons, she had at first doubted it could be for her, but after reading it several times was obliged to admit that there could be no mistake. The lady, not anticipating a refusal, had sent her own carriage, which was very luxuriously appointed.

Mrs Calverdon's house was tall and narrow, turning a bone-white face to the world, and unlike so many homes at that festive time, it had a cold dismal look. Here were no brilliant ornaments and bright lights, the bustle of gatherings planned, gifts prepared and feasts roasting. If Mina had not known the house was in occupation, she would have assumed it had been deserted for the winter.

Attentive servants admitted Mina very quickly to the presence of the lady of the house, who was sitting in an armchair before the library fire. There was an armchair immediately facing Mrs Calverdon and Mina imagined that that was where she was intended to sit, but instead, the servant drew up another chair for her and ushered her to it. After performing the introductions and ensuring that she was comfortable, the servant departed and left the two ladies alone. The room was silent apart from the whisper of flame. It was warm, insulated by heavy aged books, and hung about with paintings, one of which, above the fireplace, was a portrait of a young man.

Mrs Calverdon was about fifty years of age and dressed in mourning. Her face had the pale drawn look of someone who avoided the open air and bore sharp lines of grief but few of laughter. Her eyes appeared to be fixed on the empty chair that faced her and at first Mina wondered if she was blind, but then, with a little sigh, Mrs Calverdon turned her head to gaze upon her guest.

'Miss Scarletti,' she said softly, 'I am so grateful that you have come at what must be an inconvenient time.'

'Think nothing of it,' said Mina.

'I should explain the reason for my urgent request. I had invited another lady here to assist me and she agreed to come, but I am sorry to say that at the last moment she advised me that she can no longer attend or help me in any way. This is most distressing, since what I hope for is best attempted today. I have read correspondence in the newspapers which state that you are a psychic sensitive with remarkable abilities. It is to you, therefore, that I must turn.'

Mina hardly knew what to say. She had no abilities of the kind suggested and always denied such allegations, but since Mrs Calverdon was clearly a very unhappy lady, it seemed cruel to simply say so and depart.

'Perhaps you could tell me what it is you require?'

'Of course. I am sure you have already noticed this portrait. It is a fine likeness of my son, Roland.'

Mina looked again at the painting, which depicted a good-looking youth with brown curly hair and a cheerful smile.

'Yes, it is excellent. He is very handsome.'

'I must ask you.' Mrs Calverdon leaned towards Mina, eagerly, the firelight reflected in her eyes. 'Do you see him anywhere else in this room?'

Mina looked about her, but the other pictures were of landscapes. 'I am sorry, I do not.'

'You must try harder. Open your eyes fully. It may take time. Perhaps, as I am his mother, it comes more easily to me.' She nodded to the empty armchair. 'There. Do you not see him? He sits there. I see him so clearly.'

Mina looked at the armchair again, but to her it was obstinately empty.

'Do you see him there all the time?' she ventured cautiously.

'Not always, but very often. When he lived, he liked to sit there with his books of a winter night. During the year he is like a cloud, grey and soft, but I see his form and I know it is he. As Christmas draws near he becomes brighter, clearer, more solid and natural. I see his dear face and all the colours of his hair and clothes. It is almost five years to the day he was so cruelly taken from me. Such a good kind boy, the finest son any mother might wish for! And you do not see him?' she added plaintively.

'I am sorry, but I cannot. Does anyone else see him?'

Mrs Calverdon shook her head. 'My servants think I am mad, of course, but they say nothing, even when I talk to Roland. And he talks to me. I can see him speaking now; his lips move.'

'Do you hear him as well? What does he say?'

'Ah, now that is the thing that eats at my heart! I cannot hear him, neither can I interpret what his lips say. I had hoped that the other woman I wrote to with her extraordinary gifts would have seen him just as I do, perhaps even hear his words. And you say you do not hear or see him?' She didn't wait for a reply but sank back miserably in her chair as if she wanted it to swallow her.

Mina, seeing that there was nothing she could do to help the unfortunate lady, wondered what other comfort might be available to her at what others considered to be the season of good cheer. 'Mrs Calverdon, are you all alone here?'

'I choose to live alone. What of it?'

'Are there friends who might call on you to keep you company? Do you have family? Other sons? Daughters?'

Mrs Calverdon did not respond to the suggestion of either friends or sons, but at the word 'daughters' an expression of great anger and distress passed across her face.

'You have daughters? Can they not call or invite you to visit them?'

There was a long pause. 'One,' said Mrs Calverdon reluctantly, almost spitting out the word.

'Where does she live?'

'What does that matter?'

'Because Christmas is a time when families gather together. I can see from your manner that there has been a rift between you and your daughter, but surely this is the season when such wounds can be healed. Would she not come and see you?'

'No. And I don't want to see her. She is the reason —' Mrs Calverdon stopped and bit her lip. 'Are you sure you don't see Roland?'

Mina, not having the heart to leave the poor woman alone with her misery, searched for some means of easing her. 'I cannot see him, but it might help me to do so if you could tell me more of your history. I do want to understand.'

Mrs Calverdon fastened her eyes on the empty armchair once more. 'Oh, Roland, my dearest boy, I wish you could tell me what I should do!'

'I cannot imagine that Roland would want to see you so unhappy.'

'No. He would not.'

'If you can bear to talk about it, how did he pass away?' Mina asked.

Mrs Calverdon looked up at the portrait. Tears had formed in the corners of her eyes and they glowed in the firelight like tiny flames. 'It was the night of a grand Christmas Eve ball. The weather was very wet. Evelyn — my daughter — was eighteen and it was her first grand ball. She was very excited, as I suppose was natural. She didn't want to be late. I was indisposed, but Roland said he would go with her. He loved his sister very much. The last thing he said to me was that he would care for and protect her. At first I thought the accident was the driver's fault, but others who saw the carriage pass said that they heard Evelyn urging him to go faster, even though it was unwise to do so as the road was slippery. The carriage overturned. Roland flung his arms about his sister to save her from harm. She suffered not a scratch. Roland's neck was broken.'

'And you blame your daughter for his death?'

Mrs Calverdon's face was distorted into a mask of tragedy. 'Of course I do! It was her fault! Her fault that I sit here alone with only the ghost of my son for company. Oh, please tell me that you see him!' she begged.

'I do not, and I suspect that only you will ever do so. It is a mother's love, a mother's pain and loss that places his image before your eyes.'

'But why can I not hear what he says?'

'Perhaps because you don't want to hear it. Mrs Calverdon, I can't tell you what your son is trying to say. No one can. Only you who love and understand him can know that. You don't need to read his lips, you don't need to hear his voice. All you need is to search within yourself. That is where the true answer lies, not with spiritualists and mediums.'

The stricken woman was weeping openly. 'Do you really think so?'

'Yes, I do. You said that Roland was a good kind son. He loved you, he loved his sister. Close your eyes and think of him as you knew him in life. If he could truly speak to you now, what would he be saying?'

There was a long silence as Mrs Calverdon composed herself and wiped tears from her face, then she placed her hands over her eyes and a sigh welled up from the depths of her body, making her whole form shiver.

'Oh, the dear gentle boy! I never heard him utter a word against another soul! Many years ago, when he was a small child, he had a favourite toy which another child, a friend of his, played with and broke. I thought he would be angry, but instead he told that child that he forgave him and the two stayed friends.' Her hands fell to her lap and she gazed on the empty chair again. 'Is that what you want, Roland? Is that what you truly want?' She uttered a sudden gasp. 'I can see it now! I can see it! "Forgive" he says! "Forgive!"'

Mina seized the moment. 'Can you do that? Can you forgive your daughter? For the sake of your son? In his memory?'

Mrs Calverdon, the words choking in her throat, nodded.

'Then write to her. Ask her to come and see you. Or visit her. Is she married?'

'Yes. Two years. I have a grandson. I have never seen him.'

'I am sure they will welcome you.'

Mrs Calverdon gave a little moan. 'Roland, my child! My boy!' She stretched out her arms. 'He is fading. He is grey like mist! But he no longer speaks. He only smiles. Such a beautiful smile. He is —' she sobbed — 'he is gone.'

'He has not gone,' said Mina soothingly. 'He will always be in your heart. When you lose those you care about, they live on in you. I know that too well myself.'

It was some while before Mrs Calverdon felt able to speak again, but when she did, she clasped Mina by the hand. 'You are right. Christmas should be a time of joy, and for five years it has brought me only pain. Roland would never have wanted that.' She looked up at the portrait, and this time she smiled. 'I have so many good memories.'

'And there will be new ones. Do you have a portrait of your daughter?'

'Yes — I — put all the family pictures away, but I still have them. Would you like to see them?'

'I would, very much.'

Mrs Calverdon rang for the servant. Refreshments were brought, a note was written to be sent to her daughter, and for the rest of the evening the two ladies sat by the cosy fire looking at albums of pictures and sharing stories of loved ones, and the happy memories of Christmases past.

Want to discover more ghostly Victorian mysteries?
<u>Start reading the Mina Scarletti Mystery series now!</u>

Connect with Linda Stratmann!
<u>Facebook/BooksByLindaStratmann</u>
<u>Twitter:@LindaStratmann</u>
<u>lindastratmann.com</u>

A NOTE FROM THE EDITOR

Thank you for taking the time to read this crime fiction short story collection from Sapere Books. From deadly cases in Victorian London to modern crime capers in Ireland and Wales, we hope there is something in this anthology to suit everyone!

The authors of the stories in MIDWINTER MYSTERIES have all written full-length crime novels, either currently published, or soon to be published by Sapere Books. If you have enjoyed their stories, please do get in touch with them directly via their social media links at the end of their stories, or sign up to the **Sapere Books newsletter** for updates on their latest releases.

If you enjoyed the collection it would mean a lot to us — and the authors — if you could leave a review for it on **Amazon** and **Goodreads**, and if you are interested in becoming a crime fiction reviewer for Sapere Books, then please do get in touch with our Marketing Director, Caoimhe O'Brien via her email address: **caoimhe@saperebooks.com**.

Thank you once again for reading and I hope these stories have got you in the mood for the Christmas season — hopefully one full of comfort and joy, and not theft and murder!

Amy Durant
Editorial Director
Sapere Books
saperebooks.com
Twitter: @SapereBooks
Facebook: SapereBooks

Sapere Books is an exciting new publisher of brilliant fiction and popular history.

To find out more about our latest releases and our monthly bargain books visit our website: **saperebooks.com**

Made in the USA
Columbia, SC
07 December 2020